"For starters," Thomas said. "Why don't you tell me who you are?"

The woman wiped her tears, looked him dead in the eye and sighed. "I'm– Well, I'm Darcy Simmons and I'm–I'm Jesse's daughter."

Daughter? What? Jesse didn't have any kin that Thomas had ever heard of. Jesse had always been all alone...

The woman–Darcy–had hardly gotten the words out when her fancy smartphone rang.

She looked at the phone and frowned. "I don't know that number."

Still, she touched the screen to accept the call and lifted the phone to her ear. She was so close that Thomas could hear every crazy word of the call. The oddly distorted voice filled the room.

"Oh, Darcy, honey, you're just as lovely as your mother, but you do have your daddy's eyes... And you also have something of mine. I'll be coming around soon to get it back. You can either cooperate when I see you, or you can end up like your dear old dad. Either way, I get what's mine. See you soon."

Kit Wilkinson lives in the heart of Central Virginia, where she works full-time as a French and English teacher and overtime as a mother of two. A graduate of the University of Virginia and the University of Tennessee, Kit loves to study, learn and read. She finds through writing she is able to do both with a purpose, while creating something new in the process. You can visit her website at www.kitwilkinson.com.

Books by Kit Wilkinson

Love Inspired Suspense

Protector's Honor
Sabotage
Plain Secrets
Lancaster County Target
Lancaster County Reckoning

Love Inspired

Mom in the Making

Visit the Author Profile page at Harlequin.com.

LANCASTER COUNTY RECKONING

KIT WILKINSON

HARLEQUIN® LOVE INSPIRED® SUSPENSE

Recycling programs
for this product may
not exist in your area.

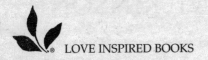 LOVE INSPIRED BOOKS

ISBN-13: 978-0-373-45712-0

Lancaster County Reckoning

www.Harlequin.com

Printed in U.S.A.

Behold, I stand at the door and knock.
If anyone hears my voice and opens the door,
I will come in to him and dine with him and he with me.
—*Revelations* 3:20

To Dad, thanks for sharing your love, most especially
your love for story and books. I miss you.

And to my sister, Elizabeth, my biggest fan and
most dear to my heart, the Lord shines through you still.

ONE

Thomas Nolt spotted the bright red car the second he entered the clearing. It made for such an odd sight on his neighbor's land, in the middle of their Amish community, that he pulled up on the reins of his gelding. The sudden stop of the horse threw the weight of the satchel his grandmother Ruth had loaded up with baked goods and preserves for his "Uncle Jesse" against his back.

Not really an uncle but his close neighbor of twenty years and considered part of the Nolt family, Jesse Troyer had asked Thomas to come take a look at his well at lunch. So it seemed a bit odd that someone else was visiting at the same time. Not that it was unusual for Jesse to have any visitors, but most of his acquaintances drove the typical Amish horse and buggy—not cars. And certainly not a fancy, brightly colored automobile like this one.

To be sure, Jesse had not always been Amish. Thomas had been just a child when Jesse had joined their community twenty years earlier, but he remembered how hard the man had worked to embrace the plain life and leave his *Englisch* ways behind. Ever since, Jesse pretty much stuck to his friends in the Ordnung. He had never mentioned keeping in touch with anyone in the *Englisch* world.

Thomas wanted to tell himself that it was nothing to

worry about. In all likelihood, the red car's driver was a tourist who had gotten lost and had stopped at Jesse's home for directions. Christmas was approaching and tourists seemed oddly fascinated by the simple, minimal decorations with which the Amish commemorated the holy season. Yes, there was surely nothing ominous about the appearance of the red car at all. And yet Thomas could not deny that he felt strangely unsettled.

His eyes moved over Jesse's house, and he finally realized what seemed off. It was a cold December day with a biting wind…and yet no smoke rose from Jesse's chimney. The old man was home. Jesse's little bay-colored Morgan horse was enclosed in her paddock and his buggy was parked, as always, next to the house. So why hadn't he lit a fire? An emotion washed over Thomas. It was a feeling deep in his gut—a feeling that something was wrong.

He nudged King into a gallop over the open field, only slowing when they'd reached the back of the house. Thomas dismounted with one smooth swing of his leg and rushed around to the front porch, where he came to a full, screeching halt.

"Who are ye?" The words flew out of his mouth before his brain could rephrase them into something more courteous. He took a slow step back as if he'd encountered a rattlesnake. It might as well have been seeing as what stood in front of him rattled his brain. It was a young woman. A young *Englisch* woman with modern clothes and styled hair and a face painted to a glossy fashion magazine's idea of perfection. She was petite but looked agile and adept.

"Who are *you*?" she countered in a flat tone. She looked down at the bench and snatched up a fancy little handbag, which she stuck under her arm as if to keep it safe.

This was no tourist. If she was simply passing by, she would have assumed Thomas was the home's owner, and would have launched into her explanation of where she was trying to go and how she'd gotten turned around. Her expression made it clear that she knew this wasn't Thomas's house. And that meant she was looking for Jesse specifically. But why? She looked at him with equal reservation. Tension exploded between them.

At least he belonged there. Thomas crossed his arms over his chest.

From the top of her coiffed head to the bottom of her designer boots, she looked as out of place as a chicken swimming in the river. "Are you lost, ma'am?" he asked, hoping he'd read her wrong. "I can tell you how to get back to the highway."

"I'm not lost," she retorted.

Thomas scratched his head. "Well, then, if you don't mind me asking, what are you doing here?"

"I don't see what concern that is of yours." Her voice was edgy.

His eyes locked on hers. "Well, I'm a neighbor of the folk that live here and I've never seen you before. I am just looking out for my neighbor."

Thomas noticed that the front door had been cracked open. "Have you been inside, ma'am?"

"No. Of course not."

"Then why is the door opened?" Thomas didn't mean to accuse her, but Jesse was a responsible man—he wouldn't have left his door open like that. He *would*, however, have left his door unlocked. Doors were rarely bolted in their close-knit community and Jesse in particular was known to keep his home accessible. He was unbothered by visitors at any hour who wanted his help or to borrow a tool or simply to sit and share a cup of tea. If this woman had wanted to let herself in, she could have easily done so.

"The door was opened when I got here, which was about

a minute before you did. I didn't touch it. I didn't even look in. I was just…" She stopped and pressed her glossed lips together. She shook her head and glanced at her watch. "I was just waiting for Jesse. We had an appointment. You don't happen to know where Mr. Troyer is, do you?"

"Jesse was expecting you?" Thomas could feel the muscles in his face tightening. *Why?* Why would Jesse have a meeting with an *Englisch* woman? He wanted to ask but held that thought at bay. "I assume he is inside. Did you knock?"

"Of course I knocked." She backed out of the way as he moved toward the front door. "Since the door was already opened, I thought maybe he stepped around back or something. I was going to go check when you arrived."

"Jesse?" Thomas called.

He pushed the door open wide and stepped inside the small cottage. She followed him in as if she feared to be left by herself on the porch. Although what he found inside might have been worse. It was chaos. Everything inside had been turned upside down. Furniture toppled. Drawers emptied. Jesse's belongings had been scattered from one end of the home to the other. Behind him, the tiny woman gasped and threw a hand over her gaping mouth.

"Ach! Had ye seen this?" he asked.

"No. I told you I didn't go inside." Her gray eyes were wide with alarm.

"And you're alone? You came here alone?" he asked her.

"Yes," she said. Her voice was breathy and low. "Like I said, I just got here. I was supposed to meet Jesse at noon. I—I was a few minutes late. I knocked on the door and called inside. No one came, and then you were here."

Thomas didn't know whether or not to believe a word she was saying but the astonishment in her voice sounded genuine. "And you haven't seen anyone coming or going?"

"Just you." Her gaze flowed from one end of the room to the other, surveying the damage. "Whoever you are. You never told me your name."

"You never told me yours." Thomas unloaded the sack of food on his back. It landed with a clunk in the center of Jesse's kitchen table. He looked back into the woman's dark gray eyes. "I'm Thomas. Thomas Nolt. I live next door."

She seemed to take that in for a long moment, avoiding eye contact. But that was typical. Being Amish, Thomas was used to *Englisch* people either staring for too long, or just the opposite—not wanting to make any eye contact.

He frowned at the scattered mess. Of course, break-ins did happen, even in Amish communities from time to time. But they were rare, and usually there were teenagers involved. Jesse was a sixty-year-old widower with no children. Not exactly a typical target for a teenage prank. And as for robbery as a motive, he had no electronics, no money, no jewelry.

The strange woman bit her upper lip nervously as she moved around some of the clutter and farther into the house. "Who do you think did this?"

"I was just wondering that my—"

A faint moaning sounded overhead from the loft.

There was someone else in the cottage. Thomas looked at the woman. "Stay here."

Thomas raced up the back stairs. "Jesse? Is that you?"

The *Englisch* woman didn't listen to him. She was on his heels, on the narrow staircase to the loft.

At the top of the stairs, Thomas paused. More chaos. The loft looked much like the downstairs. Completely trashed. He took a few wide steps over the debris and made his way to an odd-looking lump in the corner, from where he estimated the sound had originated. *Jesse!*

The old man lay in a heap on the floor. His face was

swollen. His lips bloodied and bruised. Jesse had been beaten. And from the looks of it, nearly to death.

His wounds looked fresh and in some places were bleeding out. And worse, Jesse wasn't moving. Thomas dropped down to his hands and knees and grabbed the old man's hand. Thomas had seen men after fights a few times. He'd never seen anyone roughed up like this, as if the people who'd attacked him hadn't cared whether he survived or not.

"It's okay, Jesse. It's Thomas. I've got you. Just rest. You're going to be fine."

The woman had slowly edged her way around the loft. She let out a horrible squeal as she saw Jesse on the ground. "Oh, no, no, no. Jesse. No."

She dropped to the floor to get closer to the wounded man. Her body moved in waves of silent sobs.

"He's not dead," Thomas said, although he could barely detect the old man's pulse. "Hang on, Jesse. Hang on. Help is here." He looked to the woman. "You have a phone in that fancy bag of yours?"

Still crying, she scrambled through the little bag, plucking out a shiny smartphone. Her hands were shaking so badly that she had to try three times to enter her pass code to unlock the phone. For efficiency's sake, Thomas grabbed it from her and called 911. He gave thorough directions to the dispatcher. He also asked him to notify the local clinic, which was even closer than the fire department and the EMS. He hoped they would make it in time.

As he spoke, the *Englisch* woman placed a small pillow under Jesse's head and a blanket over his torso. She touched Jesse's hand and whispered something low into his ear. *Who was she?*

He held the phone out for her to retrieve. Thomas's own hands were trembling, too. It was all he could do to control his emotions. He was filled with a mixture of horror and anger. What had happened? Who would do such a thing to a kind man like Jesse? And why?

He looked at the woman, wondering if her sudden and strange appearance had anything to do with the beating Jesse had taken. Thomas sighed aloud. He had to refocus his thoughts.

He had to remind himself that God was in control. His anger would solve nothing and it certainly wouldn't save Jesse, which should be his only concern at the moment.

The woman took the smartphone from his hand. "How long will it take someone to get here? Maybe you should carry him to my car? I can get to a hospital faster than waiting for an ambulance. Right?"

"Wrong."

"What?" She looked back at him with surprise. "Of course that would be faster."

"Maybe faster but not better. He may have broken bones that need to be stabilized before he can be moved. I don't want to cause any more damage than has already happened. I'm not moving him."

"Right. Right. You're right. I'm sorry." She stood back and put her hand to her forehead. She was trembling like a leaf. "But what can we do? We have to help him."

We? Thomas took off his hat and put it back on his head. It was something he did when his thoughts or emotions were getting away with him. A little trick his father had told him about when he was very young that reminded him to take a deep breath and pull himself together.

"For starters," he said, "why don't you tell me who you are."

The woman wiped her tears and swept her bangs carefully away from her face. At first, Thomas thought she hadn't heard him or was once again avoiding an answer.

But then she looked him dead in the eye and sighed. "I'm... well, I'm Darcy Simmons and I'm—I'm Jesse's daughter."

Daughter? What? Jesse didn't have any kin that Thomas had ever heard of. Yes, he'd been married. But that had been years ago. In fact, his wife had died before Jesse had moved to Willow Trace. Jesse had always been all alone...

The woman—Darcy—had hardly gotten the words out when her fancy smartphone rang out a series of loud beeps that was apparently her ringtone.

She looked at the phone and frowned. "I don't know that number."

Still, she touched the screen to accept the call and lifted the phone to her ear. She was so close that Thomas could hear every crazy word of the call. The oddly distorted voice filled the room.

"Oh, Darcy, honey, you're just as lovely as your mother, but you do have your daddy's eyes... And you also have something of mine. I'll be coming around soon to get it back. You can either cooperate when I see you, or you can end up like your dear old dad. Either way, I get what's mine. See you soon."

The phone slipped from the woman's hand. Her head dropped back and her eyes fluttered as her legs collapsed under her and she fell toward the floor.

TWO

The giant Amish man caught Darcy under the arms just before she hit the floor.

"I'm okay. I'm okay." She still felt light-headed and shaky, but she was able to straighten her legs and stand on her own...mostly.

Thomas backed away quickly, as if touching her had stung his hands. "What was that about? That phone call?"

"I have no idea. I told you I don't know that number." Darcy's head swirled. "I have no idea who that was or what he was talking about. The voice didn't even sound real. It was more like he was using some kind of distorter."

Thomas frowned down at her, his face darkening with suspicion. "But you *are* Jesse's daughter?"

She nodded. "But no one knows that. I only just found out myself."

The Amish man shook his head up and down as if he understood her words, but Darcy felt like he didn't believe her. She could hardly blame him. She had trouble believing it herself. After years of being told her father was dead, it had been a shock to have Jesse contact her.

"Okay. Let's just concentrate on Uncle Jesse," he said.

"He's your uncle?" Did that mean this man was her cousin?

"No, but lots of people call him that around here. When I was a kid, he didn't like us calling him Mister."

"Oh." Darcy tried to slow down her breathing. It was hard to imagine this massive, intimidating man had ever been a child.

She'd rarely seen such an imposing figure, so tall and strong, dressed in black trousers and a green button-down. Dark curls spilled out from under his hat and his beard—if you could call it one—was made of thin, sparse stubble, shaved clean to the edges of his broad face. No mustache—which she had heard was the Amish way. His wide brown eyes had golden flecks around the pupils, which seemed to pulse as he stared down at her. He was a Goliath of a man, one continuous string of muscle. If he had been around earlier, whenever the attack had taken place, she doubted anyone would have touched Jesse.

Poor Jesse. She knelt beside him and held his hand. Thomas sat opposite, his eyes closed. She guessed that he was praying as she saw his lips move in silent speech from time to time. She was thankful he asked her no more questions.

And he'd been right. It wasn't long before help arrived. The EMS workers quickly strapped Jesse on a gurney and started him on fluids. She and Thomas followed the gurney to the ambulance, and watched as it was loaded inside.

On the one hand, she was thankful for Thomas's presence and his ability to answer questions she couldn't—about any medical conditions Jesse had and whether he was allergic to any medications. But on the other hand, she couldn't help resenting him just a little for knowing her own father so much better than she did herself.

When the ambulance was ready to drive away, she and Thomas looked at each other.

"I'm going to follow. You want a ride with me?" she asked.

"Are you sure?" he said hesitantly.

Was he kidding? After that phone call, she wasn't exactly keen on being alone. She nodded.

Soon, they were at the hospital. The hours blurred together as they waited for news on Jesse's condition.

Small groups of Amish men and women came through the waiting area. They would talk quietly with Thomas, glance her way once or twice then leave. Thomas stayed on one side of the room. She chose to sit at the other side. She didn't want to talk or meet more Amish people. She didn't want to explain who she was or why she was there.

And certainly she didn't want to talk about the phone call. She didn't even want to *think* about it. That hard robotic voice and the person who, unaccountably, knew her. Knew who she was. And knew her connection to Jesse. Someone who, if they really were connected to the attack against Jesse as they'd implied, had almost killed her father. The thought of it sent a shiver down her spine.

She shook away the terrifying thoughts. Right now she just wanted some news about her father. Was he going to live? Was she going to find out why everyone had lied to her for so many years? Or was Jesse going to leave her almost as quickly as he had come back into her life?

"I'm going to get a coffee. Could I get you one?" Thomas stood over her. His long dark curls, freed from his black felt hat, which he twisted nervously in his hands, sprung around his tanned face.

"Sure." Darcy reached in her bag for money.

"No. It's on me," he said. "But why don't you come down to the cafeteria with me? It will be good to sit in a different seat for a few minutes."

He hadn't seemed interested in talking to her in the

hours up to now. Why the change? Realization struck as she recalled watching him speak quietly to a doctor at the end of the hall a few minutes earlier.

"You've had news?" Darcy stood so quickly her head felt light.

Instead of answering, Thomas nodded toward the elevator bank. She followed him out of the waiting area, into the elevator, then down the hall to the cafeteria. She wanted news of Jesse. Even if it meant talking to this stranger.

"Thank you for the ride to the hospital," he said, handing her a hot cup.

"Of course," she said. "Thanks for the coffee."

They sat opposite each other at one of the cafeteria tables. Darcy stared into the black liquid, watching steam swirl up from the cup. She took a drink. It was bitter and stale, and as it hit her stomach, she was reminded that she'd skipped breakfast and hadn't had a chance to eat lunch.

"So, how is he?" she asked at last. She had a feeling that the news wasn't going to be good or he would have already told her.

"They are operating on him." Thomas's voice was quiet and strained with emotion. "But…apparently there's some internal bleeding and they are having a hard time stopping it."

"So what does that mean?"

"They are going to try another procedure. If it works, it will stabilize his condition."

"And if not?"

"If it doesn't work…then they don't expect him to live through the night."

"What?" Darcy had not expected good news but she hadn't expected anything as bad as this. "That can't be. There must be something we can do. Maybe we need a second opinion?"

She pushed away from the table, fighting tears of rage and fear. Thomas grabbed her gently by the wrist. His hand felt strong and warm as he pulled her back to her seat.

"Dr. Jamison is one of the best ER doctors in the Northeast. He and his team are doing all they can. It's in God's hands."

Seemed more like Jesse was in this doctor's hands, not God's. And she wondered why one of the best doctors would be working all the way out here. But she couldn't muster the energy to ask.

Darcy slumped back into the chair. She felt so out of place and helpless. And confused. It wasn't like her at all. "It's just that… I don't know how to deal with all of this. I just found out my father has actually been alive all this time and now he's…well, beaten almost to death. I just wish there was something I could do to help. And yet, I don't even know if it's my place to help or if Jesse would even want me to."

"It's okay. It will all get sorted out. These things take time. The doctors are doing everything they can to save him. Plus, I know Jesse pretty well and I can tell you for sure and certain that he is a very strong man."

"I just hate doing nothing. Just sitting here and waiting."

"Well, there is something you can do. Something we all can do."

"What's that?" She lifted her head.

"We can pray."

"Oh." Pray? Really? Darcy looked away and tried to keep her facial expression neutral. It wasn't that she thought praying was stupid. It just wasn't for her. "Of course… I guess I was thinking of doing something more active and practical, maybe, like finding who did this to him."

"*Ja*, well, one thing at a time. Plus, I'm sure the police have been notified about the beating. They will look for whoever is responsible. There is no need for us to go anywhere until Jesse's condition is stable." There was a lovely lilt to his voice. He had a faint accent that she hadn't noticed before. "If Jesse were awake, he would be praying. That I am sure of. But you would know that, of course, since you're his daughter, *ja*?"

Darcy swallowed hard. She put her elbows on the table and surrounded the warm cup of coffee with her hands. "I only met Jesse a few weeks ago. And we mostly talked about me." She regretted that now.

"But you are his daughter?" He stared out at her from under a wisp of dark curls. He tilted his head, focusing hard on her face. "Truly Jesse Troyer's daughter?"

Strange emotions flowed through her. "I'm afraid so. And I understand your surprise."

He grinned, revealing a beautiful set of white teeth. "*Ja*, it is a surprise. But truly, if I hadn't known Jesse for the past twenty years, I would not question ye so many times. You have his eyes, for certain."

In spite of herself, Darcy smiled a little, remembering meeting Jesse for the first time and feeling that shock of recognition when faced with those unusual dark gray eyes she'd seen in the mirror every day of her life.

"But it is just that, well…he never mentioned you," Thomas said.

"No one ever mentioned him to me, either." Darcy rubbed her temples, thinking back to when she'd first met Jesse at the coffeehouse just a few weeks ago. "I grew up with my grandparents—my mother's parents—in northern Virginia. I was told my parents had both died in a car accident right after I was born. There were newspaper articles and everything, showing the crash. Turns out half of it was a lie. The crash did kill my mother…but my father was alive all along.

"I mean, I don't have any legal documents to show you

as proof of paternity. Jesse talked about getting them if I wanted him to. But at this point I wasn't really sure where this whole thing was going. And anyway, he had proof enough for me—pictures of me as a baby. And pictures of my mother. Pictures of the three of us together. And he had this locket. My mother's locket. She always wore it. It's around her neck in almost every picture I've ever seen of her."

Darcy lifted the beautiful silver necklace off her collarbone to show him. Thomas looked at the locket then turned away. It was impossible to tell what he was thinking. Whether he believed her or not. His stoic face hid his emotions. Calm strength was all he allowed her to see. But she didn't really care what he thought of the situation. Thomas was just a neighbor. She was Jesse's daughter, his own flesh and blood.

After a long moment of silence, Thomas looked back at her with faraway eyes that were hazy with sadness. "Jesse did talk about your mother. He spoke of her often to me."

"Yes, my grandparents talked about her all the time. She was amazing," Darcy said, thinking of all the comparisons they'd made when raising her. Comparisons she'd never lived up to.

Thomas sighed. "So how did you find out? How did you and Jesse meet?"

"Jesse wrote to me." She smiled. "An old-fashioned letter. He told me who he was and he sent some pictures. One of them was a picture I had seen before in my mother's things."

"That must have been strange."

"Yes, at first. But then I became curious. I asked my grandparents about it. About him." A sharp pain stabbed at her heart. "But they wouldn't tell me anything, except that my mother was dead and that it was his fault. They told me if I wanted to go down that road of getting to know my father, that I would have to do it alone."

"I am truly sorry." Thomas's eyebrows pressed together, his brown eyes examining her carefully. "Family… Well, we should always be able to count on family."

"It's okay. My grandparents have always been a little… different." *Cold.* "But actually what they said only confirmed to me that Jesse was telling the truth. So I met with him. And when I saw him, I knew. Jesse is definitely my father. I just wish…" *I'd known about him…*

Tears started to well in her eyes. Thomas reached across the table and patted her hand.

"Hey, now, I am certain that he had a reason for not getting in touch with you sooner. And if I know Jesse, and I think I do, then he had a very, very *gut* reason." He gave her hand a quick squeeze, then slid his hand back to his side of the table. "Jesse—your father—is a *gut* man. A man of God. And he is strong. I am praying that God will let him stay with us a bit longer. We cannot change the past, but you can still have a future together as father and daughter."

The tears started to spill over. Darcy tried to hold them back. She didn't want to cry in front of this stranger. She covered her face with her hands.

Thomas stood. "We should go back now. The police will probably be here soon."

Darcy felt the blood drain from her face. She did not want to talk to the police. She couldn't imagine that she knew anything which would be helpful. And what if no one believed that she was Jesse's daughter? "Oh…but I don't know what to say to them…like I told you I don't have any real proof that he's my father."

"It is going to be okay, Darcy. Just tell them what you told me."

"Do they know about the phone call?"

"I haven't spoken with them yet. But I hope you plan to tell them. It may help them find out who did this. Isn't that what you want?"

"Of course it's what I want. But how can I explain what the man said to me? Not to mention, no one really knows I'm Jesse's daughter. What if Jesse doesn't want anyone to know?"

"I don't think you can keep being Jesse's daughter a secret any longer." He smiled. "You have nothing to fear from Jesse's friends. I know that much. Which makes me wonder why—"

"Why he kept it a secret?" she said, finishing the question for him. "I don't know. It's not a topic you just jump right into the first time you meet your father."

And now he might die and she would never know.

Darcy closed her eyes. Thomas was right. There was no escaping her identity any longer. She was the daughter of a man who had been attacked for hiding something. And the man who had committed—or commissioned—the attack was now after her, unless she turned over something she knew nothing about. It was all so cryptic and horrifying. She didn't know what they wanted and if Jesse didn't wake up and give it to them then...

What did they have planned for her?

THREE

"Chief McClendon." Thomas shook hands with the Lancaster head of police. They had met before during another stressful time in Thomas's life, when his own niece had been murdered. And while most Amish didn't have much to do with government or law enforcement agencies of any sort, Thomas had a healthy respect for the chief. McClendon had always kept his family's confidences and respected their boundaries. Right now, Thomas had a sense that the chief would be helping him again through whatever was going on with Jesse and Jesse's long-lost daughter.

"This is Darcy Simmons." Thomas moved his eyes quickly between her and McClendon. "And she is…well, she is Jesse Troyer's daughter."

"Oh." McClendon turned to Darcy, taking in her fancy clothes. "I guess you left the fold."

Darcy looked taken aback.

"She was not born or raised Amish," Thomas answered for her. "Jesse came to the Ordnung later in life."

"Oh, I see." McClendon frowned. "So I understand Mr. Troyer was badly beaten?"

"We hope he will pull through, but it's too early to know his status for certain," Thomas replied quickly, wanting to keep Darcy focused on the positive.

She looked well past the point of exhaustion. Her hands shook. Her eyes were swollen. She seemed so horribly… alone.

"I'll need to ask you a few questions about your…well, about Jesse," McClendon said to Darcy. "And about what happened earlier today."

She nodded.

"You add in anything in that might be helpful," McClendon said to Thomas. "I understand you were both there?"

"I arrived first," Darcy said, explaining how she and Jesse had planned for her to come at noon. "When I got there no one answered at the door, and I noticed it was cracked open. Then Thomas came. We went in together and found that someone had torn the place apart. Then we discovered Jesse upstairs on the floor. Thomas called 911. And then—then I got this strange phone call."

Thomas exhaled a sigh of relief, pleased that she'd overcome her hesitation and decided to share the truth with the police chief.

"How do you mean, *strange*?" McClendon asked.

Darcy quoted the caller verbatim. McClendon scratched his head. "And you have no idea who would have sent you a threatening message?"

"No." She shook her head.

"You didn't recognize the voice?"

"It was modified. Computerized. It didn't sound natural."

"Did either of you see anyone coming or going from the area around the house?"

They both shook their heads.

"Did you see anything unusual or missing?"

"It was impossible to tell. The place was wrecked."

"Right. We sent a team over to Mr. Troyer's place to investigate. But they won't know what or if anything is missing. Then again, based on this phone call you're telling me about, it seems likely that the caller didn't find what he wanted at Jesse's home."

Thomas nodded. That made sense. Whatever the man from the phone call was after, he'd probably tried to get Jesse to reveal where it was first. When that hadn't worked, he'd tried searching the house for it himself. When that failed, he'd threatened Darcy. But how had he known about Darcy? That was still a puzzle.

"So, you're from Philadelphia?" McClendon asked her.

"Originally, I'm from Virginia. But I've lived in the Philadelphia area since college. I work as a buyer for Winnefords department store."

"You live alone?"

She nodded. "I have a small town house in the suburbs."

"You work in the city?"

"Mostly. I travel to New York a lot."

McClendon flipped through his notes. "Now, what was your relationship with your father?"

"We…didn't have a relationship until recently."

The chief looked up at that. "None at all? Was it a custody issue?"

"No, it was… To be honest, I'm not really sure what it was. I was raised by my mother's parents. They blamed Jesse for my mother's death, so maybe that's why they told me my father had died when I was a baby. They didn't want anything to do with him."

"And when did you find out the truth?"

"About a month ago. Jesse sent me a letter, and we met for the first time a week later."

"Did you tell anyone that you were coming to Willow Trace today? Did anyone of your acquaintance know about Jesse and your recent discovery that he is your father?"

"No. No one knew I was coming. Only Jesse. And I

hadn't told anyone about him contacting me, other than my grandparents. But they didn't want to discuss it."

McClendon looked to Thomas, who hoped the questions were nearly over. Darcy looked ready to collapse.

"She's told you everything as it happened," Thomas said, hoping to head off any more questions.

"Has she?" the chief asked. "So you can confirm what she's said about the letter and meeting with Jesse? He told you about his daughter?"

Thomas flushed. "Well…no, actually, today was the first I heard of it."

"Do you consider yourself close to Mr. Troyer?"

"*Ja*, of course. We have been neighbors for twenty years."

"And he never mentioned a daughter? Not even in the past few weeks?"

"No," Thomas admitted. "He has spoken of his wife and I knew she had died, but there was never mention of a daughter." Thomas couldn't deny that the situation was strange. There were so many things that didn't make sense. And the only people with answers were the threatening man from the phone call and Jesse, who might never wake up again.

But Thomas believed that Darcy was being honest with them. Her shock and horror at Jesse's attack had been real. And so was her fear at the phone call.

"It must be related—the beating and the phone call," Thomas said. "Don't you think? It was almost like the caller was watching us. Like he knew exactly when to call."

"So what's your theory on why anyone would want to beat up a nice Amish man and threaten his daughter?" McClendon asked.

Thomas shook his head slightly. For that he had no answer. "I cannot even imagine who would want to hurt

Jesse. He's just a sweet old Amish fellow who minds his own business."

"You said he's been your neighbor for twenty years. Where did he live before?"

Thomas took off his hat and scratched his head. "I don't recall. That would be a question for the bishop."

Could all this be tied to Jesse's past? Jesse's life before he came to Willow Trace? But that was so long ago. Even if he had enemies from decades in the past, why would they come to trouble him now?

Thomas shifted his weight and kept one eye on the door. He was on the lookout for his friend Elijah. Earlier he had asked the ER staff to notify not only the bishop and leader of the Ordnung about the beating, but also his friend, who had spent many years in the *Englisch* world working as a police detective before returning to his Amish roots. Thomas hoped Elijah's experience with police investigations could help them.

McClendon continued questioning Darcy. "Do you give the police permission to track your incoming phone calls? In the case this happens again?"

"Of course. You can *have* my phone if that helps you find whoever did this to Jesse," she said, handing over her phone.

Thomas saw Elijah Miller enter through the waiting room doors and walked over to greet him. He met his good friend with a hearty handshake. "Are you a sight for sore eyes. Here. Come. McClendon is speaking to her."

"Chief," Elijah said as they joined Darcy and McClendon. "And you must be Miss Simmons. The whole Ordnung is praying for Jesse. And I'm here to help in any way I can."

Darcy seemed confused as she looked over Elijah and took in his Amish dress but somewhat *Englisch* mannerisms and speech, which Thomas had learned that his friend could turn on and off depending on what the situation might call for.

"Eli is a former detective," Thomas explained.

"Well, I'm just a farmer now, Miss Simmons. But I worked for ten years on the force in Philly, before coming back home," he said.

Darcy nodded.

"I just came from the cottage," Elijah said. "There was a team of investigators. So far, they seem to have no leads on who attacked Jesse. Jesse lived plain. Very plain. There was nothing in his home that anyone would want to steal. But there was a business card with Miss Simmons's personal information and number. We found that on the floor with a few papers and some old pictures."

"Well, that could be how they got your number," McClendon said, turning to Darcy. "But that doesn't explain how they would know you're Jesse's daughter."

"There was a letter there from Darcy," Elijah said. "I didn't read it. I think it was marked into evidence with the photos."

"Photos?" Thomas repeated. "I can't imagine Jesse having photos. It's verboten."

"Forbidden," Elijah said, translating. "But if they were his only tie to his daughter for all these years maybe he kept them anyway. Or maybe he just got them recently."

Still, pictures? Thomas's head spun with doubts and confusion. This did not sound like the Jesse that he knew.

"In the morning," Elijah continued, "a few of us are planning to meet up at Jesse's and help put the place back together. It's quite a mess."

"I'll be there." Thomas shook Elijah's hand.

"Miss Simmons—" Elijah tipped his hat "—I hope you hear some good news very soon."

"Thank you." Darcy nodded and finished up answering a few more questions from the chief.

Thomas walked Elijah from the waiting area.

"Thank you for coming." He shook his friend's hand. "It is *gut* to have someone who can help us make sense of these things. Not that I can see any sense in the harm that was done to Jesse. He was really beat up. And you heard about the phone call to Darcy?"

"No." Eli looked grim. "What phone call?"

Thomas filled Elijah in on every detail. "If only Jesse could tell us what this is all about."

"I think Darcy should take that threat seriously after what happened to Jesse. But what could Jesse have that would be worth nearly killing him over?"

"That is what I keep asking myself over and over," Thomas said. "Do you remember when Jesse moved here? You and I wanted to go to his cottage every day after chores and play baseball or lawn croquet."

"I remember." Elijah laughed then stopped abruptly.

"Do you remember if he ever said where he came from?"

"No. I don't guess I ever really thought about it too much. He always just fit in. Like he'd been here forever."

"But he wasn't," Thomas said. "And he's got a full-grown *Englisch* daughter to prove it."

"Maybe the Elders know. They must know something about his past from when they accepted him in to the Ordnung. I could ask my father."

"Would you? But would he even be able to tell you anything?" Thomas wondered if that was the right thing to do. "I mean it's one thing for us to know he has a daughter. It's another for us to know the whole story behind their past and their separation."

"I'm sure if Jesse thought that his daughter was in danger, he'd want us to help, no?" Elijah patted him on the back. "And we can help a lot more if we know more."

"But if we interfere then are we leaving it up to God?"

"God will work through all of us. We will either get the answers or we won't."

"Okay. I'll see you at the cottage at noon tomorrow."

Elijah smiled. "All will be well."

All will be well. In God's time.

Thomas returned to the waiting room. McClendon had gone. Darcy had reseated herself on the other side of the room and did not look as if she wanted company. He could respect that. She had gone through a lot in one day. He imagined Darcy was barely holding it together.

Thomas slumped down into a seat that he decided looked the least uncomfortable. He lowered his hat over his eyes and let his chin rest on his chest.

Secret daughter? Jesse attacked and left for dead? Threats that he has something that belonged to someone else? Thomas just couldn't wrap his head around it. It was as if the Jesse he'd always known was someone else entirely. Images of Jesse swam in Thomas's head as he drifted off to sleep…

"Hey, man, wake up."

Thomas sat up fast. There was a horrible pain in his back and neck. Dr. Blake Jamison of the ER stood over him, looking like he hadn't slept in days. Thomas checked the clock on the wall.

"Seven thirty?" He stood and rubbed his neck. "Last I saw, it was midnight. I guess I fell asleep."

"Glad somebody did." Blake glanced over toward Darcy. "Is that Jesse's daughter? I have news."

"*Ja.* Come." Thomas shook the ache from his stiff bones

and led his doctor friend across the large waiting area. He hoped and prayed that Blake had good news.

"Darcy, this is Dr. Jamison." Thomas cleared the sleep from his voice. "Blake is the head of the ER here. He's been with Jesse."

A brief smile brushed over Darcy's lips. The lipstick had worn away and her lips were no longer stained with color. Plain and unpainted, they looked even lovelier to him than before. She shook hands with Blake. "So, how is Jesse?"

Blake rubbed a thumb and forefinger over his scruffy stubble. It was clear he'd been at work for hours. "Well, he's still with us. He made it through the night. The last procedure seemed to stop the rest of the internal bleeding."

Thomas let out a sigh of relief.

"I get the sense that you led with the good news," Darcy said shrewdly.

Blake gave her a tired smile. "You'd be right. I'm afraid not all of my news is good."

"So what is the bad news?" she asked.

"Jesse has slipped into a coma."

FOUR

A coma? Thomas was thankful Jesse had lived. But for Darcy's sake, and for the sake of Jesse's continued safety, he sure wished he could ask his old neighbor a few questions. From the look of disappointment on Darcy's face, Thomas guessed she was thinking the same thing. How were they going to get to the bottom of this without Jesse's help?

"A coma?" Darcy repeated. "How long will that last?"

"I can't say," Blake answered. "But this can happen when recovering from such trauma to the brain. In many cases, the patient is able to eventually make a full recovery."

"So he *will* wake up?"

"I can't make any promises, but we certainly hope so. There's a very good chance, and many of his indicators look positive. Still, he won't be out of the woods completely even after waking up. There was a lot of hemorrhaging and we won't be able to gauge the full extent of the damage until we can communicate with him." Blake looked at Thomas.

"So...what? What does that mean?" Darcy dropped her arms by her sides, demanding the rest of the news.

"There is always some potential for brain damage. He

may end up losing some or all of his cognitive and motor skills, and it's very possible his memory will be affected."

"So he won't remember who he is? He won't remember me? Or Thomas?"

"Every case is different," Blake said, trying to console her. But Thomas knew what Blake was really saying was that he had no idea what was going to happen to Jesse. And Thomas could see Darcy's tiny light of hope extinguishing. He couldn't imagine how she felt, reconnecting with her father after all of these years only to run the risk of losing him again so soon.

"Doctors have to tell you all of the possibilities," Thomas said, trying to sound casual. "It doesn't mean that's what will happen. God will decide what will happen to Jesse."

"So you've said." Darcy's expression soured. "But isn't there anything you can do medically to help him heal faster or better? To wake him from the coma?"

"Unfortunately no," Blake said. "His body is already doing what it needs. It's trying to heal, to live. He's breathing on his own. We just have to wait now."

"So he stays here? In this hospital? Can I move him to a hospital in the city? Closer to me?"

"Moving him right now..." Blake shook his head. "Well, that could set on a temporary decline in body function and when he's already functioning at the lowest level, that would be taking a very unnecessary risk. We should avoid anything that would stress or strain his system more."

"Can I see him?"

"Of course you can," he said. "Anytime you like."

Darcy nodded. "How about now?"

"He's in the ICU," Blake said. "Room 11."

"Thank you, Doctor." She started toward the door, but

turned back to them. "Thomas, may I join you and your friends at Jesse's later today? I'd like to help clean up."

"You would be most welcome," Thomas answered with a nod.

Blake and Thomas watched her move away toward the elevators.

"Why don't you go home and get some rest?" Blake put a hand on Thomas's shoulder.

"I was going to say the same to you." Thomas tried to muster a smile but the heaviness on his heart wouldn't allow it. "You are working yourself too hard, Blake, but thank you. Thank you for fighting so hard for my friend. I know you are doing all you can to help Jesse."

"He's a tough old bird," Blake said. "But he was beaten up like I've rarely seen. And I've seen more than a fair share of beatings working in the ER."

Thomas shut his eyes as he thought of the state they had found the old man in. The pain he must have been in. At least now Jesse could not feel the pain. He could be thankful to God for that.

"It's good you found him when you did," Blake continued. "Without blood and other fluids, I don't think he would have lasted much longer…"

"Then he must live," said Thomas. "And I pray that he does. Even apart from his value to the community and to me, it would be so sad for his daughter to lose him now, when she only just found him again."

Blake's eyes looked intrigued under the shadow of exhaustion. "What do you think of Miss Simmons?"

Darcy Simmons? Heat rose to Thomas's cheeks as he remembered the feel of her soft hand and the way her long brown waves framed her sweet face. "I—I think she is scared and confused. And…I think she is in a lot of danger."

* * *

Darcy stayed with Jesse for most of the morning. He looked so small and weak and old, lying there lifeless in the hospital bed, with tubes running in and out of him. The nurses said he was blessed to be alive. But he hardly looked it.

She wished he would wake up. She had so many questions. She no longer believed anything her grandparents had told her as a child about her parents. Was her mother really killed in a car crash? Why had Jesse started a life with the Amish? It was clear from all the photos of the past that Jesse had not been born Amish. Why hadn't he stayed in the non-Amish world and raised her? Or at least taken her with him?

There had to be reasons for his choices. There had to be something that caused him to choose this path—a path that had not included her in his life. She tried not to let her questions and confusion cause anger toward her grandparents. But it was hard not to feel betrayed by them and all the lies. She'd probably be upset with Jesse, too, except that he looked so helpless lying there all but lifeless in the hospital bed.

Please wake up, Jesse. Please tell me what happened. Tell me who did this to you and what they want.

Darcy hated to leave Jesse but she was determined to get to the cottage and help clean up. Maybe, just maybe, there would be something there that would tell her more about her father—or at least give her a clue as to who was after him. And now her.

Darcy called a close friend and colleague who was kind enough to use a spare key to her town house and deliver a change of clothes and her makeup bag to the hospital. After breakfast, Darcy felt revived with a clean suit, fresh makeup and some food in her belly. She headed out to

Willow Trace, driving through the beautiful back roads of Lancaster County. Her friend had asked her lots of questions when dropping off the clothes, which Darcy had answered merely by saying that a close family member was in a coma and she'd be away from work until further notice. Hopefully, that wouldn't be long. Funny, though, she thought as she passed an Amish man driving a horse-drawn buggy that was moving at a snail's pace compared to her, how time seemed to move slower here. Even with all that had happened in the past twenty-four hours.

When Darcy drove up in front of the cottage, there were already several Amish buggies parked in front. And there was Thomas. He was seated on the front porch, head down, a large book in his hand.

"Good morning," she said.

He looked up at her. "Good day, Miss Simmons. You look all cleaned up and fancy."

Heat rose to Darcy's cheeks. She looked down at her designer suit. "I guess it's a little dressy for cleaning."

"We are just finishing up," Thomas said. "It is time for lunch."

"Oh. I'm so sorry. I should have come earlier." Darcy was truly disappointed. She had really wanted to help. She had wanted to be a part of this. She had wanted to see Jesse's home and feel closer to him and his friends. The wave of emotions made Darcy shift her weight over her heels. Life had taught her that depending on anyone made her vulnerable to getting hurt. She couldn't allow herself to get attached to Thomas or the others in this community just because they were being kind. Maybe she should have just stayed at the hospital.

Thomas stood, folding the book closed. A Bible, from the looks of it, which he tucked under his elbow. "Come. There are people who would like to meet you."

She followed him into the small living space, which was all tidied up. There were two women inside, along with Elijah, Thomas's friend whom she had met at the hospital, and one other elderly man. All of them were Amish.

The two women were dressed similarly in homespun dresses, dark aprons and thin white caps set over their hair, which was parted straight down the middle, then tucked up and hidden away in a tight nest on the back of the neck. Darcy felt awkward in her stylish pantsuit and heels. But the ladies didn't seem to pay her or her clothes any mind. They were all smiles, happily humming as they finished their work.

"Miss Simmons, how is Jesse?" Elijah asked as he approached her. "Any change?"

"No," Darcy said, shaking her head. "Though that's not necessarily a sign of trouble. Dr. Jamison said he didn't expect there would be any change today. And he is stable. So that is good."

"We will hold a prayer gathering for him," the older of the women said as she turned to her. She was completely gray headed but had the same warm golden-brown eyes as Thomas. "I am Nana Ruth, Thomas's grandmother. You must be Miss Darcy. I think it is *wunderlich* that Jesse has a daughter. I just—"

"Nana…" Thomas glared at the old woman.

"*Ach*, Thomas." Nana held her nose up defiantly to her grandson, who towered over her by more than a foot.

"It's nice to meet you, Mrs. Nolt." Darcy offered her hand to Thomas's grandmother.

"Just call me Nana. Everyone does. And this is Hannah, Elijah's wife."

"Nice to meet you," Darcy said to the other woman, who was close to herself in age. Elijah's wife had flawless skin, shimmering green eyes and a look of genuine sympathy in her expression.

"They were teenage sweethearts," Nana explained. "Reunited by—"

"Nana," Thomas interrupted again, this time whispering something to her in their Germanic language.

Again the old woman dismissed Thomas's unsolicited guidance with a wave of her hand. "I was just going to invite her to the prayer gathering."

A change in subject was definitely in order. "Wow. This place looks great," Darcy interjected. She didn't want to be rude to the woman who had worked so hard to clean Jesse's home and who had been so kind to her already, but Darcy did not want to go to a prayer gathering. She didn't even know how to pray or if she even could. Faith had never been a part of her life. In any case, even if changing the subject had been her goal, the compliment was sincere. The transformation of the cottage was stunning. The home had been completely cleaned and organized. "It's so warm and homey."

"Just like the man who lives here." Nana glared back at her grandson. Darcy had to hold back the urge to laugh at the comical exchange between Thomas and his grandmother.

Darcy looked to the older man who sat nearby. He'd seemed uninterested in the conversation, but now rose and moved toward her.

"This is Bishop Miller. He's one of the Elders, or leaders, of our Ordnung," Nana explained. "He's also Elijah's father."

Darcy nodded at the man who was slow to make eye contact with his piercing blue eyes. There were no smiles from this person. No handshake. Yet he did not seem harsh, simply solemn. He looked like a man who carried a lot of weight on his shoulders. He stopped just a few feet from her and stood silent.

"It's very nice of you all to do this for Jesse," she said. "So very kind. I'm sorry I wasn't here to help."

"You had a long night. You must be exhausted," said Nana.

"Which is why we'd like for you to join us at lunch at Nolt cottage," said Hannah.

They didn't wait for her answer, but swept through the front door as quick as a second. Only Thomas and the bishop stayed. Thomas still held the Bible in his hands. She wondered if he took it everywhere with him. And why did its presence in his hands make her so uncomfortable? She'd seen plenty of Bibles in her life.

"Bishop Miller would like to speak with you, if that's okay," Thomas said.

Darcy nodded to him as a wave of dread washed over her.

"Then just follow the bishop to our place," Thomas said. "It's not far. About a mile or so."

She nodded again and tried to swallow down the dry lump that had formed in her throat.

The bishop remained behind as Thomas exited. It was obvious he had something to tell her. Had something changed in Jesse's condition since she left the hospital? She knew it was unlikely—the hospital had her contact information—but she was too worried to be rational. Her pulse spiked as she feared the worst of news.

"You know something about Jesse?" Darcy asked, trying to be brave.

"About his past, yes," the old man said. "Just a little. But I will share what I have been told as my son thinks it is important for you and the police to know."

"The police?" Darcy could feel her heart pounding

against her ribs. So this past might have something to do with Jesse's beating and her phone call? Did he also know why Jesse had abandoned her? Did she even want to know?

Bishop Miller cleared his throat. "When Jesse came here he was a broken man. A man running from many things. He was very scared. But he was also searching— for God and for the forgiveness that can only come from the Lord. And he opened his heart and found peace."

"Until yesterday?" Darcy asked.

He nodded.

"What was he running from? From the people who beat him? From the law? From…me?"

Darcy tried to swallow again, but her tongue felt glued to the roof of her mouth.

"He was not running from you, child, but from himself. He made many mistakes, Miss Simmons. Although it is not for me to judge." The bishop remained solemn but his tone was kind. "And please know that Jesse has had to pay dearly for his past decisions through great loss and sacrifice."

"What sacrifice? Looks to me like he came here and lived a pretty great life…"

"His sacrifice was you. And your mother."

"My mother? What do you know about my mother?" Darcy fell back into one of the upholstered chairs. None of this made her feel any better. Only more confused and sick inside.

Bishop Miller locked his sea-blue eyes on hers. "From what I was told, it all began when your father helped put a man in prison many years ago—a very bad man. Now that man has been released."

The phone call. The voice. The man who was coming after her. The man who'd already viciously beaten Jesse. Darcy's head was spinning. It felt as if all the blood had drained from her body. She tried to breathe and calm herself down, but it was like some invisible force had gripped her chest. "What did this man do? What has this got to do with my mother?"

"This man… He killed your mother."

FIVE

"Why, Darcy, you've hardly touched your lunch," said Nana Ruth as she cleared away the plates.

"I had a late breakfast," she explained. Thomas watched Darcy stand and begin to help Nana and Hannah clean away the dishes. He knew the real reason she hadn't touched her lunch. On the way from the cottage, when Darcy had stayed behind to talk to the bishop, Elijah had shared with Thomas what the Elders knew about Jesse Troyer's past.

Thomas supposed he shouldn't feel so mixed up about what he had learned. After the beating and the phone call to Darcy, he should have expected that Jesse had some dubious connections. Still, it created a cloud of mistrust to discover that Jesse had kept secrets for all these years. For Darcy those mixed emotions must have felt even heavier.

He glanced through the kitchen window. In his office in the stables, where he managed his business of raising and training horses, he'd stowed away Jesse's Bible, which he'd taken from the cottage. He was going to take it to the hospital the next time he went to visit Jesse so he could read to him. But now, he felt compelled to share it with Darcy. She should be the one to take it to the hospital and share God's word with her father. Maybe it would give her some peace in all of this confusion. By the look on her face, she could certainly use some.

"Your home is lovely." Darcy brought him a cup of coffee that Nana had poured out.

"Danki." Thomas felt a brief grin slide over his lips. He took the coffee from her hands, thinking how this woman was not quite what he had thought when he first saw her on Jesse's front porch. Fancy and sharp-witted, yes. But there was something softer there, too, although Thomas guessed it wasn't a side of her that she was comfortable revealing to many people, especially to a stranger like him.

"Well, if you like the old house, Miss Simmons, please allow me to show you the even older stables." He glanced over to Elijah. "Eli and I were just heading there to look at the filly."

Eli raised an eyebrow at the unexpected invitation, but followed Darcy and Thomas out of the white clapboard home toward the great red stable.

"So your grandmother lives on one side of the house and you on the other?" Darcy asked.

"When the house was more crowded, we definitely needed the space," Thomas said, thinking back to a time not so long ago when his brother's child and wife had lived there under his roof, dependent on his protection—protection he'd failed to give. "Now it's just the two of us. Frankly, I don't know how Nana keeps up the place all by herself."

"That's why Nana is always on the lookout for a new granddaughter-in-law." Eli slapped him on the back.

Thomas clenched his teeth. He knew his friend meant no harm, but somehow the comment rubbed him wrong. To redirect the conversation, he started to explain to Darcy that Hannah—Elijah's wife—used to live with him, along with her stepdaughter, Jessica, when Hannah was widowed by his older brother, who'd died in a buggy accident. And so it was really Eli's fault that Nana had lost her helper, when he'd come back to town to investigate the case of Jessica's murder and married Hannah. But the memory was so bittersweet. As happy as he was that his friend and his sister-in-law had found love together, the losses of his niece and brother weren't happy topics. After all, the whole point of taking Darcy to the stable was to lift her spirits, not add to the weight of what she already carried.

Thomas led Darcy and Eli through the aisles. "These are the Morgan breeding mares. On the other side are the draft mares. I have two stallions, which are housed in a separate stable on the far side of the property. And this— this is Gilda. She was just born two weeks ago."

Darcy looked over the stall door, down at the little bay filly, who tried to put her nose over the door to greet them.

"Oh, my, she's so sweet." Darcy smiled. And Thomas thought he saw at least a little of the weight from her shoulders lift. "Can I pet her?"

"Ja. Ja," he said. "She's very friendly. And already used to people. She's going to make a great driver."

He and Eli watched Darcy pet the playful filly, who snorted and nipped at Darcy's hand. "I've never really been around animals much. My grandparents wouldn't let me have a pet."

"It's sort of a mandatory experience around here." Eli laughed.

Darcy's smile slipped a little.

"I have something for you," Thomas said. "It's in the office."

"For me?" Darcy looked stunned as she followed him into his small office.

He lifted the Bible from his desk and placed it into her hands. "This is Jesse's. I found it on the table when we first started cleaning. I was going to take it to the hospital and read it to Jesse. But then I thought that he would want you to do that."

"Oh." Darcy looked frozen for a moment, then she finally extended her hands to take the great book. "I'm afraid, like the animals, I don't know much about the Bible, either."

She held it delicately in her hands, as if it was made of glass. Thomas felt a lump form in his throat. Had he gone too far? He had only meant to make things better.

"What would I read to him?" she asked.

"Just trust your heart." Thomas smiled.

She nodded. "Jesse did share some verses with me in a letter. I guess I could look those up."

Eli reached for the Bible. "Really, you can't go wrong with any part of it. For example, sometimes I'll just flip it open…"

As Elijah turned the pages, a note fluttered out from the book and fell to the floor.

Thomas reached for it and unfolded the small letter, his eyes glancing quickly over the message. Then his heart sank to stomach. He looked up at Darcy. "We need to call the chief."

Darcy pulled at the ends of her hair. How much more could she take? She wasn't sure. The note had been addressed to her to give to Jesse. It had been meant to terrorize them both. The man who had left it wanted her to know that he was coming for what Jesse had stolen. And if they wanted to live, they wouldn't get in his way. It had been signed W.W. She agreed with Thomas that they needed to call McClendon. She needed to tell the chief what Bishop Miller had told her about Jesse's past, too. Hopefully once he had all the information, the police chief would be able to piece together what was going on and stop this W.W. from hurting anyone else.

Darcy hurried from the stable to her car, where she'd left her phone in her bag. Her hands were shaking. Another threat and in a Bible of all places and... Where was her phone?

She searched her clutch bag, which was sitting in the passenger seat. The phone wasn't there. She looked under the seats. It wasn't there, either. She knew it wasn't in the Nolts' home. She hadn't taken her purse or the phone inside.

Darcy's mind flashed back to her enlightening conversation with the bishop. She remembered how the shock of his words had caused her to fall back. She had dropped her bag into the chair. Her phone must have fallen out then. It was probably right in the seat where he'd delivered the news that her mother had been murdered and the killer was now out of prison and on her trail. Now, thanks to the note in the Bible, she had yet another reminder of just how close that killer was.

She looked around, reminded of the isolation of the Amish farm. The cottage was only a mile away. It wouldn't take long to go back and get it.

She hopped into the driver's seat, her mind still spinning with all new information. Her grandparents had always blamed her father for her mother's death—for the car crash that Darcy had always believed killed both of her parents. They had lied about her father dying. But were they telling the truth when they said it was her father's fault? Had they known their daughter was murdered? And that her father had helped send the killer to prison? *Murder... Killer...* The words made her cringe. What else had everyone lied about? Had she ever known the truth about anything? Darcy felt like she didn't even know who or what she was anymore.

Darcy passed through the woods separating Jesse's land from Thomas's. The cottage looked desolate as it came into view. Jesse's horse wasn't even in the field. Probably taken to a neighbor's while Jesse was in the hospital. The thought of others pitching in to help in different ways touched Darcy. Jesse's friends and neighbors were so loyal and devoted. Darcy wasn't even sure who her neighbors were. And she was certain that if she'd been the one in the hospital, there would not have been a constant flow of visitors like there had been for Jesse.

She pulled up in front of the cottage, leaving her car running. Grabbing her phone wouldn't take a second. She jiggled the door open and headed over to the chair where she'd been sitting. The phone was nestled between the arm and the seat cushion. That was a relief.

She tucked the phone into her jacket pocket. But as she began to turn, the front door suddenly slammed behind her.

Darcy jumped at the sudden sound, but tried to calm her nerves as she reasoned that it was simply a drafty house and that a change in pressure had caused the door to shut.

But a change in pressure where? And why? She turned toward the kitchen. Was there a back door that had opened? She spun back around. Everything looked in place. She was worried over nothing. She just needed to get back to Thomas's. The sooner the better.

As she stepped toward the front door, something fell in the kitchen. The clank of a tin pot hitting the hardwood floor reverberated through the house.

Her heart froze. Darcy couldn't breathe. Someone else was in the house. She took a step back. She looked left. She looked right. She saw nothing.

She hurried back toward the open door, but a figure appeared in her periphery.

She was not alone.

SIX

Inside the barn, Thomas was pacing, trying to make sense of why he'd heard Darcy's car drive away. He hadn't joined her when she left the barn because he'd thought she was just stepping out to grab her phone—she hadn't said anything about departing yet. Darcy didn't need to be going anywhere alone. "I thought she meant her phone was in the house."

"Me, too," Elijah agreed. "Do you have your business phone?"

"Of course. It is still in the buggy we took this morning to Jesse's. I'll go get it."

Thomas jogged out to his buggy, which was parked on the other side of the stable. He would have offered his phone earlier but Darcy had been so keen to get her own. If he'd known she was going to drive off…

His little flip phone was tucked away inside the console of the buggy. It still had some power. He brought it back to Elijah. "I don't know her number."

"Call McClendon," Elijah said.

It took a few minutes but Thomas finally got the chief on the phone.

"Miss Simmons left here alone," Thomas said after explaining the rest of what they'd learned and the contents of the note they'd found.

"I'll call her," the chief said. "And I'll have my assistant forward you her number, as well. We can try to locate her by using her phone, too, if it's on and powered up."

Thomas disconnected.

"Maybe she's on her way back to the hospital to see Jesse?" Elijah suggested.

Thomas shook his head. "Why would she leave without saying anything?"

Thomas stared at his phone screen waiting for Darcy's number to come through. When it did, he dialed the number immediately. *What was that woman thinking, driving off without saying a word?*

Darcy's line rang and rang but she didn't answer. Thomas left a message asking her to return the call.

"Maybe she needed a minute and went for a quick drive?" Elijah offered.

"I know there could be a million legitimate reasons for her to drive off," Thomas admitted. "Maybe she saw the phone and realized she needed to call someone and drove away for some privacy."

He didn't believe a word of it. No matter what her reasoning, he couldn't imagine why she hadn't come back by now or said something to them first.

Thomas felt his heart jump when his phone rang in his fingers. "Darcy?" He lifted the phone.

"No. It's the chief. We can't get her to answer," McClendon explained. "But we were able to track the phone."

"Where is it?"

"Fourteen-oh-one Waking Lane."

"That's Jesse's cottage. I'm going to go take a look."

"She may not even be there," Elijah said to him. "Just because the phone is there doesn't mean the person is."

"Well, it's worth taking a look." Thomas shoved the phone into Elijah's hands. "You keep calling."

"Right," his friend said. "Take my buggy. Perry is still hitched up."

Thomas untied Elijah's horse from the hitching post and climbed inside the buggy. The trip through the woods seemed interminably long.

A large man grabbed Darcy's arm from behind. With tremendous strength, he pulled her back into the center of the cottage.

Darcy's blood raced through her veins. She screamed as she tripped backward. She braced herself and tried to whip her arm free, but his grip was too tight. Then a second man closed in on her from the other side. What could she do? They had her surrounded.

"What do you want?" The strength of her voice surprised her. She felt anything but strong at the moment. "This isn't your home. You're trespassing."

"Where is it? Where did he leave it? With you, no doubt." The voice was low and angry but with a distinct accent that she couldn't quite place. Was this the man from the phone call? Were these men responsible for the note they'd found in Jesse's Bible?

"I don't know what you're talking about, I assure you. Jesse didn't give me anything." Darcy thought of the phone inside her jacket. If she could just get the call to 911…but she'd have to do it carefully to keep her attackers from noticing. She reached her free hand slowly into her jacket pocket as her eyes darted back and forth between the two men—she needed to find a way to escape them.

"She's got a gun!" one of them yelled.

Darcy felt it before she knew what had happened. A sharp searing pain ran from the top of her head down the length of her body. She buckled to the floor. Warm blood trickled over her forehead. She fought to keep her eyes open but it was no use. Her vision blurred. Words swirled in the air above her and then the world turned black.

The cottage looked dark as it came into view, but Thomas breathed a sigh of relief when he saw Darcy's small red automobile parked in front. Thomas slowed Perry to a trot.

But the closer he got to the cottage the more Perry pranced and pulled. He sidestepped. He flung his weight around. He shook his thick, black mane and began to exhale with sharp, strong breaths.

"Easy, boy. Easy." He tried to reassure the frightened animal, but a spooked horse was hard to settle. Especially when Thomas felt a little out of sorts himself. He knew what was bothering him—he was worried about Darcy. But what had the horse so unsettled? Thomas halted the buggy and tied Perry to a hitching post in the back. He moved silently across the back lawn, nearing Jesse's cottage, then froze when a woman's loud scream echoed out of the house and across the field.

Thomas ran along the side of the house toward the front porch. Low, deep, masculine voices sounded in the cold air. Though he couldn't make out everything they said, they didn't sound familiar. And from the stray curse word he caught here and there, they certainly didn't sound Amish.

Thomas turned the corner of the front porch, just in time to see two men rush out the front door. They hopped into Darcy's running car and drove off in a red blur.

Thomas flew through the open front door and scanned the cottage. "Darcy?"

Then he spotted her lifeless body sprawled over the floor near the kitchen. Her thick dark hair was splayed around her face with bits of blood splattered around her in almost every direction.

Oh, please, Lord, no! Don't let her be dead...

For a millisecond, Thomas staggered, unable to breathe as if he himself had been struck over the head. But just as quickly he shook off the horrible surprise and made his way to her in two broad steps. Kneeling beside her, he steadied himself to check her pulse. The gruesome gash on the front of her head looked deadly and she wasn't moving.

He glanced down at the creamy skin of her delicate hands. Her painted nails glinted in the afternoon light.

He swallowed hard and pressed his fingers against her skin. *Please, please be alive. I could never forgive myself if...*

He felt her heart's rhythm stroke his fingertips. *Danki, Lord.* Danki!

He touched her cheek with the back of his hand. She didn't react. She was out cold. It was like finding Jesse all over again.

A soft buzzing sounded from the floor beside him. Her phone. He pulled it from her jacket pocket and recognized his own business number displayed on the screen. Elijah— continuing to call, as he'd promised.

"Elijah, it's Thomas. I found her," Thomas said when he answered the phone. "We need to call 911."

Darcy heard words floating over her but she couldn't concentrate on them enough to understand. A gentle hand on her forehead pressed a damp cloth against her hot skin. Her eyes fluttered. Light struck her like a club against her skull. Pain radiated from her head all the way down to her fingers.

"Hey, she's coming to," a voice said above her. A voice she didn't recognize.

Slowly, Darcy squinted and gazed up. A slender, blonde woman stood, looking down with concern. The woman wore nursing scrubs and her hair was neatly braided into one long strand, flipped over her shoulder. She was pretty and natural. Her deep blue eyes looked sharp and intelligent.

Darcy glanced over the room, recognizing Jesse's home. She was on the couch. And there were two Amish men standing by the woodstove. She knew them—Thomas and his friend. They had had lunch together. They had been at the stable. Thomas had shown her that adorable baby horse. Then what? Everything after that was a foggy— and painful—blur.

The throbbing in her head intensified with the light and movement and sound of voices. She closed her eyes and willed the horrible ache to go away. It hurt to think.

"Hi, Darcy. I'm Abigail. Abigail Jamison. I'm a nurse and I'm taking care of this head wound of yours until EMS gets here. Then we will get you to the hospital."

Hospital. Jesse. Beating. Bible. Message. Phone. The progression of thoughts strung together one by one until she remembered what had happened. Images of two huge men flashed through her pain-filled mind.

"You have a serious head injury," the nurse continued. "And probably a concussion. Is there someone we can call for you?"

Darcy felt sick from the horrible pounding in her head. She wanted to vomit, but she didn't think she could bear the pain of moving her head in order to relieve the nausea. It hurt even to think. "No. Please, don't call anyone. I'm fine. I just need to…" *Go home and forget this place. Forget Jesse. Forget this nonstop nightmare I can't wake up from.*

"It's okay. Just try to be still. I hear sirens. The emergency crew must be close. You're going to need a doctor to stop that bleeding. It's under control now, but as soon as you move it will start back up again. I know it hurts."

Darcy closed her eyes again. She felt exhausted, but too adrenaline charged to relax. She could hear Thomas and Elijah speaking to each other, whispering in a language she did not understand. Pennsylvania Dutch, most likely. The soft sounds soothed the edges of the sharp pain. "Thomas…" she said, trying to sit up, wanting to ask if he'd seen those men. But moving made her head spin. She dropped back against the pillow, and Thomas stepped up to her side.

A gentle smile cracked over his dark face. "Glad to see you awake and talking. You've had us worried ever since you went out to get your phone and did not come back."

Someone had attacked her. Fear seized Darcy's whole being. "Yes, I did. I remember. When I went to the car, I realized my phone had fallen out and I came here to find it. But…"

She closed her eyes and turned her head away from him. The nausea was overwhelming. The ability to keep her stomach from rebelling grew weaker and weaker.

"Just let her rest." The nurse shooed away the two men.

"There—there were men in Jesse's house. They attacked me," Darcy told the blonde. "Did Thomas see them?"

"He did. He's called the police. Now, you just rest," Abigail said.

"You talk like they do," Darcy said, her mind swirling in and out of the moment, not sure how to describe the accent the woman shared with the two Amish men.

"I'm Elijah's sister. And I'm Jesse's friend, which means I'm your friend." She turned the wet cloth on Darcy's head. "I also happen to be a nurse. I have a clinic nearby. So

Thomas called me to come and help make you comfortable while we wait for the EMS."

Darcy tried to speak but couldn't. Tears slid from the corners of her eyes. She gasped for air before the words finally emerged. "I don't know what they want from me. I don't know how to make this stop."

Thomas was back at the hospital. He'd come with Abigail. While doctors patched up Darcy, he decided to visit Jesse. The old man lay in front of him, lifeless. His status had not changed, for better or for worse. Thomas touched his friend's cold hand. A tear trickled down his cheek. He could not help but think about what life might be like without Jesse. He was much more than a friend. More than a neighbor. In many ways, Jesse had been like a second father to him after his own had passed away. He didn't want to lose Jesse. He'd already lost too much.

"I heard you were here," Dr. Blake Jamison said as he stepped into Jesse's room. "No change, but Jesse's holding on. He's strong. We just have to keep waiting."

Thomas hadn't heard his friend enter. Quickly, he dropped his head and wiped the tears away.

"Darcy is ready to go home," Blake continued. "But McClendon is here and wants to talk to her. And to you. They're waiting for you downstairs in a conference room. I'll show you."

Thomas nodded and followed Blake to a second-floor conference room. He knew that he and Darcy needed to talk to the police, but after being with Jesse he found it hard to transition his thoughts back to the attack on Darcy as he entered the room. What if Jesse was lost to him forever?

Thomas shook away the dreaded thought. McClendon, Darcy and another woman were seated at the conference table. He paused in the doorway as there seemed to be some dispute between McClendon and the woman as to whether or not he should be allowed in the meeting. Before he could say anything, Darcy interrupted them.

"I want him here," she said firmly. "He can answer questions about Jesse that I can't."

McClendon and the woman accepted Darcy's decision.

Thomas walked farther into the room, focusing his attention on Darcy. "How's the head?"

"It hurts," she answered with a half smile.

Thomas could tell by her speech, her clear eyes and her attitude that she was feeling much better. He was glad. And glad he'd arrived at Jesse's when he had or she might have been hurt even worse.

"But I'll be fine. Just a mild concussion and a couple of stitches. I'm not supposed to drive for twenty-four hours, which is fine since I heard the two men made off with my car."

"Your car has been found," McClendon said. "Abandoned only a mile from Jesse's cottage. The perpetrators most likely used it to get back to their own vehicle as fast as possible. It's at the station now under examination of my forensics team. Maybe they left prints. At any rate, our guys will check it over to make sure the car hasn't been tampered with in any way before returning it to you."

Darcy smiled. "Thank you. I guess that's at least one thing less to worry about. But why would they have left their own car so far away?"

McClendon shrugged. "So that you couldn't hear them approach? Or, since Mr. Troyer is Amish, they might worry that a vehicle out front would be cause for concern."

"Hi, I'm Agent Susan Danvers with the US Marshals office." The other woman in the room stood and offered a hand to Thomas. It was clear that she did not like being left out of the conversation. "We were just discussing you, Mr. Nolt."

Thomas could also tell she disapproved of his presence. "Yes, I heard the last bit. But I'm Jesse's neighbor and closest friend. I would like to be here. Thank you."

The woman was in her midforties. She was tall and dressed all in black with a tight-fitting jacket that read United States Marshal on the left side. Her short blond hair had been purposely spiked out in every direction. He would like to believe that she was truly only interested in helping, but he noticed that she seemed overly official and self-important.

"US Marshals? Doesn't your agency transport criminals?"

"Among other things," Danvers snapped. In front of her was a large, open leather case. Its contents had been spread across the table. In her hand was an identification card, which she flashed at Thomas.

As they shook hands, Thomas caught a sense it wasn't just *his* presence that was upsetting her.

Thomas took a seat across from Darcy. Agent Danvers and McClendon began to speak at the same time. When he didn't immediately gesture for her to go first, Danvers looked over at McClendon with great annoyance.

"Excuse me, Chief." Agent Danvers's tone was snippy and arrogant. "Let me tell you what I know and then I have to be off. I have other cases to handle that aren't twenty years old."

McClendon inclined his head.

"Before Jesse joined the Amish church, he was in possession of some very valuable material."

"I thought he helped to put a murderer away?" Darcy asked.

"He did." The woman looked slightly surprised that this information was already known, but she recovered quickly and smiled at Darcy. Her expression was tight. "He was a key witness in the William Wissenberg murder trial."

"So Wissenberg is the man who killed my mother?" Darcy said.

Danvers's smile dissolved into a frown. "Your mother died during the trial in a car crash. Your father claimed that the crash was orchestrated to scare him out of testifying. Of course, the authorities were unable to find any proof of that, but your father's fear for you endangered his willingness to testify, so you, your grandparents and your father were entered into the witness relocation program."

"But why were we separated?"

"I think that was a stipulation your grandparents made," Danvers replied. "Something about them blaming him for your mother's car crash. I don't know the details. This all occurred before I came to work for the department…" She paused and pressed her lips together. "Miss Simmons, did Jesse Troyer pass along anything to you before…?"

"Before he was beaten into a coma?" Darcy looked at Danvers. She seemed to struggle with her emotions as she crossed her arms over her chest. One hand raised to the locket hanging around her neck. She rubbed the charm between her finger and thumb. "We exchanged some pictures and letters. He bought me a coffee and—"

A buzzing sound filled the small room.

"Oh, that's me," Danvers said, checking the phone hitched to her waistband. "I'll need to take this. Excuse me for just one second."

She answered the phone and left the room. Thomas felt like the front of opposition had departed with her.

"Wi-ssen-beeerg." McClendon wasted not a second before typing the name into his small tablet. "I guess that's who the W.W. on the note could be. Says here that he was released one week ago after serving a twenty-year sentence for the

murder of a private security guard. If Jesse helped put him in jail, maybe this is all an act of revenge?"

"Except revenge would only motivate one person, and there were two men who attacked me." Darcy looked over at the screen on the tablet. "And they were both way too young to be that guy."

Thomas nodded. He agreed with Darcy. The two men he'd seen leaving Jesse's house were much younger than the man who'd been released from prison.

"Perhaps, they were hired muscle," added McClendon.

Agent Danvers burst back into the room and began gathering her things. "Well, it turns out, I'm going to have to go, so let me get to the point, Miss Simmons. Your location has been compromised. So, I'm here to ask if you'd like to be relocated to ensure your safety."

"What about Jesse?" Darcy asked. "What about my grandparents?"

"We don't believe your grandparents were ever in any danger. They were only relocated because they took over custody of you," she said. "And Mr. Troyer? Well, we will see if he wakes up.

"You don't have to decide right now." Danvers snatched the large leather case into her left hand and handed a small business card to Darcy with the right. "Here's my card. Let's meet again soon." With a glare at McClendon, she added, "In private."

Darcy looked even paler than when Thomas had found her on the floor at Jesse's.

Danvers was halfway out the door, then she paused and looked back. "Call me, Miss Simmons. I can get you to safety and you can leave this all behind."

SEVEN

Darcy dropped her head into her hands as she desperately fought the onslaught of tears building. Her head spun and it wasn't just from the injury. She had been in the witness relocation program her whole life? Then who was she, really? Or who had she been? What were her parents' real names? Where had they lived? The questions devoured her. She wanted to curl into a ball and will all of these horrifying truths away. Truth was supposed to mean freedom. But these truths felt more like they were destroying everything she believed about herself and her past.

Thomas and McClendon fidgeted in their seats. They probably didn't know what to say after the whirlwind visit from Agent Danvers.

How strange her life had become. She couldn't even imagine what Thomas must be thinking or feeling about Jesse. And her. "Well, that was enlightening," she said.

"Actually, it answers a few questions that I had," Thomas said, his voice heavily coated with emotion.

Darcy suspected that Jesse must be much more than just a neighbor to Thomas. The thought made her a little jealous. She'd barely had a chance to form any kind of relationship with the man through their brief meetings—and now she might never have the chance.

"You weren't abandoned by your father," he continued.

"Nope. Stolen away by the grandparents, it would seem."

"I wonder how Jesse found you?" McClendon asked.

"And how this Wissenberg found Jesse?" added Thomas. "Do you really think this is about revenge?"

McClendon nodded. "Partially, but there must be more than that at stake here. Wiessenberg is clearly after more than simply hurting Jesse. He seems to be after whatever it is that Danvers claims Jesse had."

"*Stole* was the word used in the letter." Darcy didn't care that her tone sounded severe and unforgiving.

"Danvers asked you about receiving gifts from Jesse," McClendon continued. "And she mentioned believing that Jesse has something of great value."

"Well, he didn't give me anything like that," she said.

"As far as I know, he doesn't possess anything like that—not anymore. Jesse lives very plain. He may not have been born Amish but he lives the life to the letter," Thomas said.

"But by finding you," McClendon said to Darcy, "he has inadvertently put you in harm's way. If you don't know what these people are after then maybe you should consider what Ms. Danvers said about going someplace else where you can be safe."

Darcy didn't want to start her life all over again. Did she? What about Jesse? What about her grandparents? They may have lied to her, but they did love her in their own stiff way. She was certain of that. And she loved them.

How had all this happened? If only Jesse could wake up and tell her what they wanted, then she and her father could relocate together and live the life that was taken from them…

Thomas excused himself from the room while McClendon continued to question Darcy and warn her about her own safety. Thomas must have sensed how tired she was because he came back with a nurse. He was rescuing her again. And she was very grateful.

"You need rest." Abigail, the pretty nurse from the cottage, entered the conference room with a smile. "You're welcome to come stay as our guest tonight at the clinic. We have plenty of room."

A safe place to stay. Darcy hadn't even thought about that. Her attackers had known her phone number—she doubted it would be that difficult for them to find her address. Still, she didn't know Abigail at all. On the other hand, she couldn't drive and asking a friend to come pick her up would mean explanations that she didn't feel like giving.

"Are you sure? There could be trouble," Darcy said. She didn't want to bring her problems, her dangers, to someone else. But what else could she do?

"I'm positive. Thomas, Chief McClendon, you are welcome to join us for dinner," Abigail offered.

"Not me. Thank you. I've got piles of work," McClendon said. "But I will send a squad car by the clinic every hour through the night. No more uninvited guests for you, Miss Simmons. I'll be in touch."

"Thank you," Darcy said. McClendon nodded and left.

Thomas accepted the dinner invite but said he had a few things to do first and would meet them at the clinic later.

Darcy wanted to walk out to Abigail's car, but the nurse insisted she stay in a wheelchair.

"Hospital policy," Abigail said as they exited.

"This is awfully kind of you," Darcy told her a little later as they drove along the single-lane country road.

"Well, Jesse is like one of the Nolts. And the Nolts and the Millers are like—well, our families have been friends for ages. So that kind of makes you like family."

Darcy felt a lump the size of Kansas form in her throat. She wasn't used to all of this sentimental talk. "You and Thomas seem close."

"Ach. Ja," she said, throwing a hand in the air. "Growing up, it was hard to get away from him and my big brother. They were such a pair. Always into trouble."

Darcy tried to imagine Thomas not behaving. But it was hard to imagine him as a mischief-making boy. He was all strong, serious man. "Really?"

"Really. And Thomas instigated most of it. Nearly gave his Nana a stroke a few times."

Darcy's mind wandered quickly back to the meeting with Danvers and McClendon. "I suppose Thomas shared with you what Agent Danvers came to the hospital for. Is that why you offered for me to stay over?"

"Well, Thomas did tell me, but I would have offered anyway. You don't have a car. And even if you did, I wouldn't let you drive it. Not with a head injury like that."

"I could have called a cab," Darcy said.

"And gone where? Home alone? Thomas wouldn't have let that happen."

Thomas would not have *let* it happen? What business of it was his? Mixed feelings settled over her. On the one hand, Abigail was right. She shouldn't go home alone. Not even after that first phone call had come through, but especially not after what Agent Danvers had told her. On the other hand… "Thomas shouldn't feel responsible for me. He doesn't even know me."

"Knowing you has nothing to do with it. You're Jesse's daughter and Jesse can't look after you so Thomas feels that it's his duty. Thomas and Jesse are pretty tight. Both being widowers and all."

Thomas was a widower? That meant Thomas had been married and in love. Darcy swallowed away the strange taste in her mouth and forced a laugh. "I don't think in my adult life I've ever been called someone's duty."

Abigail laughed, too, though hers sounded more sincere.

"So, one of the other nurses told me about you and Dr. Jamison. And then I remembered reading in the *New Yorker* about your husband's search for his biological parents," Darcy said. "I never thought I'd meet someone featured in such a prominent magazine."

"Blake hates all of that nonsense. Thankfully, it's all died down since we got married."

Darcy decided that she liked Abigail. She was intelligent and married to a very wealthy man and yet she was so down-to-earth. "I like how everyone is so uncomplicated here. I don't meet many people like that. Not in my business. In fashion everyone is complicated—or pretends to be."

Abigail nodded, but Darcy got a sense she might not agree with her statement. They rode on a few minutes in silence.

"Do you have a computer I could use?" Darcy asked.

Abigail nodded. "I do. But you shouldn't be looking at a computer screen with a head injury. Your work will have to wait."

"It's not for work," Darcy said. "I want to know more about who Jesse used to be. If he testified in a trial that put someone in prison for twenty years, there has to be something about that on the internet, right? We know who he put in jail, so maybe Jesse's former name is out there to find, as well. Or even better, we could find out what these men who beat Jesse up are after."

"In that case, you tell me what to look up and I'll work the computer for you."

"Deal."

Thomas had gotten a ride home from the hospital by calling a local business that provided a sort of taxi service to the Amish. He was anxious to get home and take care of his horses. As soon as he returned, he pulled some from the fields. A few he turned out with heavy blankets. Others he led to their stalls. Then he provided fresh hay, clean stalls, water and feed for his herd. Most days, he had a teenage boy come and work for him. But today he was solo, just him and the horses. Thomas liked the time it gave him to think. To pray. And to be patient as he waited for an indication of God's will.

He was thankful he wasn't a person like Agent Danvers—attached to a cell phone, constantly talking, constantly moving on to the next thing without having taken care of the one before. But it wasn't just that endless busyness that set Thomas's teeth on edge when he thought of the government worker. Sure, she could have been a little more sympathetic when asking Darcy to consider upending her whole life. But there was something else about her that had rubbed Thomas the wrong way. Something about the way she asked Darcy if Jesse had given her anything. What was that all about? What business was it of hers what Jesse had given his own daughter?

Then again, what did Thomas know about such matters? Nothing. His life was faith, family and his four-legged friends. Not beatings, intrigue or danger.

Thomas locked up the feed room then checked on Nana, telling her that he would be eating with Blake, Abigail and Darcy. The sun had already set and Thomas decided to park the buggy for the evening. Sadie had already trotted all over Willow Trace and he had put her away for the night. Instead, he called the same car service that he had used earlier. As he was getting into the back of the driver's car, Nana came running out of the house. One would have thought the place was on fire. But she was only there to hand him some fresh baked bread to take over for the dinner. She didn't believe in going to someone else's table empty-handed.

On his way to the clinic, he passed the Miller farm, which bordered his land on the opposite side from Jesse's. He asked the driver to pull off and drive up the lane. He found Elijah out chopping wood. Elijah smiled when he saw Thomas emerge from the back of the small commuter car. Thomas quickly updated his friend on what had transpired in the conference room of the hospital.

"I can't get over Jesse being in witness protection." Elijah slammed down his ax and split another log in half.

"Well, that's what I wanted to ask you," Thomas said. "Why would Jesse go into hiding after he testified and the guy was convicted? And how would anyone have found him once he did? How did he find Darcy if they separated when they got new identities?"

Elijah stopped and leaned on his ax. "I think it makes sense after what my father told us. That Jesse blames himself for his wife's death. Whether that car accident was before or right after he testified, it doesn't really matter. If someone is powerful enough, they can have people found and killed whether they are behind bars or not."

"Hence why Darcy and her grandparents also got new identities," Thomas said. "So this Wissenberg person must be pretty powerful. Or at least he used to be."

Eli nodded.

"But how would this guy find Jesse after all these years?" Thomas said. "And how did Jesse find Darcy?"

"I don't know, but his timing sure was bad, getting in touch with her right before Wissenberg was released."

"He must not have realized it was happening. No way Jesse waited all this time before contacting his daughter just to put her in danger," Thomas said.

"The US Marshal didn't tell you anything more?" Elijah asked.

Thomas shook his head. "She did not say much. She offered Darcy a new identity. Then she left in a big hurry. I got the feeling McClendon had more questions for her. Darcy, too. But the agent wasn't going to answer them. She said she couldn't talk in front of me. Maybe I should have left the meeting."

"I'm glad you didn't." Elijah rubbed the tip of his beard. "I still have friends in the FBI. Especially one—a guy by the name of Frank Ross. You've met him. He may be able to help us fill in some of these blanks."

"I don't know…" Thomas hesitated. It was not the way of the Amish to meddle in police or government affairs. Shouldn't it be left up to God? "What if we find out things about Jesse that he doesn't want us to know?"

"I think it's far too late for discretion," Elijah pointed out. "The information we don't know is putting Jesse and Darcy in danger. We can't protect them without learning more of what's going on. Anyway, it's Jesse. And Jesse's daughter. He would want us to help, even if it meant revealing things about his past."

"She's staying with your sister tonight," Thomas said. "I'm headed there for dinner. McClendon is sending a car by every hour, in case there's trouble."

"Even more reason to get some information for ourselves. I'll call Agent Ross," Elijah said. "You go to dinner. Call me if you need me."

"I always do." Thomas smiled and returned to the back of his driver's car.

Dinner was pan-seared chicken with potatoes and fresh vegetables, served with homemade iced tea and chocolate pie for dessert. Darcy surprised herself at the quantity of food she was able to consume after having spent most of the day nauseous.

Her nerves had calmed some, but the US Marshal's unveiling of her secret life weighed on her mind like a pile of anvils. As did the agent's offer for Darcy to be relocated again.

Should she really start a new life? Never talk to Jesse again? Never talk to her grandparents or coworkers again? It seemed such a terrible price to pay, but would it be worth it if it meant she'd be safe? She was glad she had more time to think about it. With her head pounding and her mind reeling from the attack, she was in no shape to make a decision that would change her whole life.

Conversation over dinner had been light. Lots of stories about Jesse. While she couldn't repress lingering jealousy that these people had known her father so much better than she had herself, she was still grateful for insights into the kind of man he was. Abigail and Blake were the perfect host and hostess. Their home was well decorated and had every modern convenience—a great contrast to Jesse's cottage, and even Thomas's larger but still simple home.

"I can't believe how kind you are to have me over like this," Darcy said. "And it's so great that you're Jesse's doctor."

"Happy to do it," Blake said.

"But I wasn't thinking when I agreed to stay here,"

Darcy continued. "You guys are newlyweds. I'm totally imposing on you. Not to mention the chance that I could be attacked again, putting you at risk. I should get a room at that B and B I saw on the way in yesterday. It looked charming."

"It is," said Blake. "I lived there when I was working as a visiting doctor at the hospital. But we don't mind you staying here at all."

"In fact, we insist you do," Abigail added.

She had to credit their enthusiasm to their loyalty to Jesse and Thomas. They were doing this to please them.

"So, how did that meeting go with McClendon today?" Blake asked. "Any leads on who beat up Jesse and tried to do the same thing to you?"

Darcy was surprised when it was Thomas who let out a low grunt of disapproval. "That was not what the meeting was about."

Blake's eyebrows shot up. "Really?"

"Oh, my, Abigail, you haven't even told him what he's gotten himself into inviting me over," said Darcy.

"He already knew about the attack," Abigail said. "It's not going to make any difference to us that you and Jesse were part of WITSEC."

"What? Wow! That's not something you hear too often," said Blake. "Witness relocation… I would have never thought of that. Do you know why you all had to relocate?"

Darcy shrugged. "Not completely. I only know the basics. I was hoping to use your computer and do a little research?"

"Sure." Abigail stood from the table and began gathering dishes to take to the sink. Blake followed her lead. "It's in the clinic area. Help yourself but make sure that Thomas reads the screen for you."

Blake grabbed his young bride and pulled her close,

giving her a kiss. "Nurses are the worst, right? They don't let anyone do anything."

"What's that supposed to mean?" Abigail pushed him away playfully, and whipped him with the drying towel.

"The computer is through there," Thomas told her, lifting his arm to direct her.

There was plenty of information to be found online about Wissenberg. Years before, he had been the director of the Gregorian Museum of Fine Art. Then he was arrested and convicted of murder, international smuggling and fraud. One article stated that it was believed that he had illegally sold over one hundred million dollars worth of museum-quality art.

The Gregorian? That was one of the most prestigious museums in the United States, located right in the heart of the nation's capital.

The more Darcy found out about this mess, the less she really understood. How had her father gotten mixed up in this?

Thomas read the article aloud.

"'Smugglers at the Gregorian—William Wissenberg, former director of the Gregorian Museum of Fine Art, has been convicted of murder, international smuggling and fraud. He was condemned to a life sentence and a fifty-million-dollar fine for having "displaced" hundreds of important works of art over the past ten years. Sources say that his operation was so well constructed that if it had not been for the testimony of a former Gregorian employee, who was also the lead member of the Wissenberg smuggling ring, that Wissenberg would never have faced charges. Instead, he was convicted of killing security guard Kevin Loewer, age sixty-five.'"

Thomas glanced over the rest of the old article. "Director of the Gregorian? That's something. Elijah said that

Wissenberg must have been important… So, you think that it's Jesse who is mentioned at the end of the article? The former employee? The reporter never reveals his name."

Darcy let out a low exhale. "Yes. I guess he must have worked at the Gregorian, too."

Thomas tried searching Gregorian employees during that time frame matching the ten years in question, but in all of the news coverage they could find, everything seemed to be about Wissenberg.

"Thinking I was born with a different name than Darcy Simmons is pretty strange."

"A name is just a name," Thomas said. "It does not change who you are. I only knew your father as Jesse Troyer, but I can see in him the man who used to work for a grand museum. He is definitely a very educated man. I'm not surprised he did something scholarly. He is always reading. Taught me a lot. He could approach things from a different perspective that challenged me to think about why I believe what I do. And he always knows how to explain things in relationship to his faith."

Darcy felt a pang of mixed emotions, which quickly turned over to anger. "But what you just read about the employee who testified—if that's Jesse who gave the evidence against Wissenberg, then that means he was also a large part of a smuggling operation. That doesn't bother you? I know he's in a coma, and I shouldn't feel angry at someone in a coma but…"

Thomas dropped his hands from the keyboard. "I don't know who Jesse was before he was Jesse. But the man I know is a good man, Darcy. I thought of him as a second father after my own passed away. And I can't stand the thought of losing him. It does not matter what he was, or what he did. Our God forgives. And so must we."

"I'm sorry," Darcy said. "About your father." *About my*

outburst. That I'm scared out of my mind. That I don't even know who I am.

Thomas looked over at her and smiled. "*Ach*, that was a long, long time ago. But my *datt* and yours, they were good friends, too."

Jesse was still a thief and his association with criminals got her mother killed. She couldn't forgive that so easily. Darcy shook her head slightly, tears rolling down her face. "I was really looking forward to getting to know him. But now to find out that he was a thief? That he conspired with a murderer? No wonder my grandparents hated him. He ruined our family by being a part of some crime ring. How can you forgive someone for that?"

Thomas touched her wrist with his big calloused hand. Warmth shot through her skin and she stared down at her small hand under his. For a moment, she didn't feel the pain in her head.

"Do you think that maybe that's unfair?" he asked gently. "You told me yourself that Jesse never got a chance to explain himself to you. Wait until you hear his side of the story before you condemn him."

"How do you only see the good in everything?" She thought about turning her hand and lacing her fingers with his. Instead, she pulled her hand away and shook off the crazy idea. What was she thinking? She felt close to him—but it was only because of the circumstances. Once this situation was over and she was no longer in danger, there would be no reason for her path to cross the Amish farmer's again.

Thomas left shortly after, with Blake giving him a ride home. Darcy took a quick bath and settled into her luxurious guest room. But sleep eluded her. She couldn't relax. Not with all that had happened. Not knowing what she now knew. How was she ever going to accept it all?

She continued to struggle with the idea the next morning, sitting in the passenger seat of Abigail's car.

"I feel silly being babysat," Darcy said to Abigail as they pulled up in front of Nolt cottage.

"Nonsense," Abigail said. "Someone needs to keep an eye on you to make sure you don't experience side effects from your injury, and Nana Ruth absolutely loves to have company. Let her fuss all over you today. You need to rest up if you expect to get back in the swing of things. And your car should be ready by the time my shift is over."

"Are you sure? I do have a friend or two in the city. I can call one to come pick me up, and I'm sure they'd be willing to keep me company for a few hours." Darcy felt ashamed to keep depending on the kindness of Jesse's community. "I really think I've outworn my welcome."

"Don't you want to check on Jesse later?"

"Well, yes, but—"

"Then why call in someone from the city when we are all here to help you?" Abigail said—the woman knew her reasoning was sound.

"I really can't thank you enough," Darcy said. "Your kindness. Everyone's kindness here. I don't think I've ever needed it more."

But what price would they pay for that kindness? Would they get hurt simply because they were helping her? How could she live with herself if that occurred?

EIGHT

Thomas didn't have to like or dislike what he and Darcy had uncovered on the internet the night before, because he didn't dare let himself believe it. Not yet. Jesse had been his good friend—to think him anything but a good and honorable man hurt something deep inside Thomas.

More than ever he wished Jesse would wake up. Tell them the truth. Set this all straight. But he knew God would take care of things in His time, not Thomas's.

Darcy had spent the day at his home, working inside with his grandmother. He had stayed away, mostly getting his own work done. But he knew that it was about time for Abigail to come and pick her up. Where would she go? Would she stay another night at Abigail's? Had she heard anything from Chief McClendon? Had she decided to accept the US Marshal's offer to relocate her?

Thomas was anxious to hear something from Elijah and his friend at the FBI. But as Elijah always told him, calling in these types of favors took time and it hadn't even been twenty-four hours. He was glad he had work to keep him busy.

Thomas grabbed a tiny halter and took a filly out of the large pen away from her mother. She didn't like that too much but the youngling would have to learn.

He led her down the aisle, slowly but firmly, as he whispered sweet words to her. Calming words.

"You'd make a good father." Darcy's voice sounded from the front doors of the stable. "But isn't she a bit young to take from her mother?"

"No, this is good for her. She has to learn to trust humans." Thomas turned and smiled. He was glad she'd come to the stable. In fact, he had hoped that she would. With his closeness to her over the past couple of days, he had begun to grow attached to her in some capacity. It was silly. A fleeting emotion, probably born out of his loyalty to Jesse. Nothing to linger his thoughts over. He smiled at her. "What have you and Nana been up to?"

"Sewing," she answered.

"You sew?" He had not expected that. Even though she had said she worked in fashion, he had pictured her in an office, in meetings, surrounded by models and designers, not behind a sewing machine.

"Yes, how do you think one designs clothing if one can't sew?" Her gray eyes looked up at him.

She had a playful smirk on her face. He had to stop himself from staring at her, focusing his attention on the filly.

"So do you do this every day with her? Get her used to people?"

"Not every day," he said. "Not yet."

Darcy walked up beside him and reached her hand out to the baby's muzzle. The filly sniffed around her fingers then nipped at them. Darcy squealed and let out a little laugh. "She's going to bite me."

"Maybe." He laughed back. "But I don't think so. I think she likes you."

Their eyes locked for a moment. "Come. It's time to return her to her mother."

"Thomas, can I ask you something?"

"Sure. I've certainly asked you enough questions." He walked the filly to the enclosed pen with her mother.

Darcy was silent. He looked back at her to find a grim look on her face.

"Well, it's none of my business really…" She hesitated. "But I was just wondering, because Abigail told me that you…"

"She told you that I what?"

"That you were married once." She looked down and away.

"Is it so hard to believe—that someone would marry me?" He couldn't stop the wide smile that spread over his face and he laughed.

She looked up with wide eyes, her lips quickly spreading into grin that was laced with relief. "No. Not at all. I'm sorry. That's not what I meant."

"I know." He looked down at her and stepped close.

"Like I said, it's really none of my business. I didn't mean to be disrespectful but… I was curious."

"It's okay. It is a good question." He got control of his laughter and suddenly became serious again. "I was married. But it was a long time ago."

"What happened?"

"Cancer."

Darcy closed her eyes. "Oh—oh, I'm so sorry. I shouldn't have asked."

She started to turn away, but Thomas didn't want her to leave. He reached out and grabbed her gently by the wrist. "Don't be sorry. As I said, it was a long time ago. All is as God planned."

"You really believe that?"

"I do. Do you doubt it?"

"I don't know. I guess I never really thought about it.

About God." She pulled back from him. "So what's up with the beard? I thought a beard meant that you are married?"

She had changed the subject away from the topic of faith. Thomas didn't press her. God would open her eyes in His time. If she wanted to talk, God would provide the moments. He didn't have to force them.

"*Ach.* So you do not like my Amish beard?" He laughed out loud again. "It is different, no? Without the mustache?"

"Yes, it's very different."

"Once married it is custom to keep the beard. And frankly it's easier than shaving all of it every day."

"Doesn't look like you have all that much to shave," she teased.

"That is true. Just like my *datt.*"

"You must miss him."

He missed them all—all those that he'd lost. It was something he and Jesse had always had in common—loss. "Like Jesse missed your mother—and, I guess, you, too. He didn't tell me about you but as I said before, he used to talk about your mother.

"Her name was Margaret, right? He really loved her. A lot of Amish ladies have tried to catch his eye over the years, but Jesse was true to his one love. And to you."

"What do you mean?" Darcy felt like no one was true to her and especially not Jesse.

Thomas shrugged. "Just that he gave you up to keep you safe. Giving up a child—that's a sacrifice no parent wants to make. I think that may have been part of the reason he never tried to make a new family for himself."

"I'm not sure how I feel about it all. He wanted to protect me…but he left me. I should be so angry. But, mostly, I'm just confused. Why did he do those things? Why *would* he do those things?"

"I don't know." Thomas could almost see the battle

within her. The struggle to love a man who should have protected her, raised her, loved her, but who made decisions that prevented him from being in her life at all.

"And how did they find us?"

"I don't know that, either. But I suppose secrets are only as secret as the people who keep them."

"Who do you mean… Do you mean Jesse?" Darcy tilted her head.

"No. I mean the government. WITSEC should be safe. But I guess there can be corrupt people anywhere."

She took a minute to process that. Then she said, "Thomas, what am I going to do?"

Thomas paused, pressing his lips together. He wanted answers, too. He couldn't stand seeing the pain and fear in her. He wished Elijah would call with news. "Trust in God."

"Easy for you to say. You don't have people trying to…" She touched her hands to her head. "My head is starting to hurt. I think I need to sit down for a while."

"I'll walk you back to the house."

Darcy closed her eyes. She needed rest. And though she had enjoyed her time with the spirited Amish woman, spending the day with Nana Ruth hadn't provided her with much downtime. Only those few minutes in the stable with Thomas had made her forget about the problems in her life. But even that had ended when Thomas began speaking of her mother. It seemed he'd heard more about her than she had. Her grandparents had rarely spoken about their daughter, saying they found the memories too painful.

It was late afternoon now—almost time to go. But go where? Where could she go that would be safe? She felt safe at Thomas's home, but she couldn't stay there.

She could feel him so close to her as they walked back across the yard and to his house.

"Darcy…" He stopped her with a hand to her shoulder.

She turned and slowly looked up. She was so tired and he was so…so handsome. And kind. And strong. It was his strength that was most appealing.

"What is it?"

"Well, I do not know why, but I cannot stop thinking about that Agent Danvers from the US Marshals."

"Me, either. She was sort of unforgettable." The reminder of her looming decision hovered in the air.

"No. It was something she said. Something she asked you that I keep thinking about."

"About my relocation? About your neighbor being a big phony?"

"No, Darcy." There was disappointment in his eyes.

She dropped her head. She shouldn't have said that about Jesse—not to Thomas, who cared for the man so deeply.

"It was her question about what Jesse gave you."

"Yeah, well, he didn't give me anything of value. I looked at the locket. It's silver plated. It's not valuable to anyone except me."

"But what if what Jesse gave you wasn't actual valuables, but information?"

"Information? But he didn't tell me anything, either. Not even that we were in witness protection. He said very little about the past. We just talked about our lives now… and mostly we talked about me."

"But he sent you letters?"

"Yes, but there wasn't anything special in them."

"Do you still have them?"

"Yes, they're at home. But I'm telling you, there's nothing special about—" Darcy stopped as she heard the faint pulsing of her phone on vibrate.

She pulled the phone out of her jacket with trembling fingers. "I don't want to answer it."

"But you should. We need to know what the caller wants if we're going to keep you safe. Remember the police are tracing your calls."

"You answer it then." She held the phone out to him. Thomas pressed the screen to answer the call.

"Hello."

The line went dead.

NINE

"You think it was the same person that called before?" Darcy asked later that evening, as she drank a cup of tea with Thomas and Nana while waiting for Abigail. Nana had brewed it to help calm her nerves, but so far the tea had done little to help her mind settle.

Thomas shrugged. "I don't know but whoever it was didn't want to talk to me."

Maybe, Darcy thought, unsure whether or not she should be grateful that the call had ended before it had really begun. On the one hand, they needed all the information they could get. But on the other hand, she couldn't take hearing that horrible distorted voice again.

"I'm sure Abigail will be along any minute now," said Thomas. "Where are you planning to stay tonight?"

"You can stay in *Dawdi* house with me," offered Nana.

Darcy's eyes shot over to Thomas. By the way he was looking at his grandmother, she guessed he wasn't too keen on that idea. Neither was she.

"I need a change of clothes, so I thought first I'd drive home," she said, hoping that would be good enough for Nana. But it wasn't.

"Well, you can't do that all by yourself," Nana said. "If these men know who you are, they might know where you live. Thomas, you'll have to go with her. And then if you're not going to stay with us or with Abigail, then you'll just have to spend the night with the Millers."

"Or at the B and B," Thomas offered. "And I'd be mighty obliged if after we gather your things at your home, you would drive me to the hospital. I would like to visit with Uncle Jesse for a bit."

While Darcy turned the idea over in her mind, Thomas stood and walked to the back door. "Here's Abigail now," he said, "and another car following her."

Darcy turned and glanced out the window behind her. "That's my car. I thought she was going to take me to it, not bring it to me?"

A few seconds later, Blake and Abigail walked through the back door.

"I hope you don't mind," Abigail explained. "The car was ready early so Blake and I went on a lunch date to pick it up, went back to the hospital and finished our shifts, then thought we might as well just bring it straight to you."

"Thank you," Darcy said, taking the key from Abigail.

"We also wanted to offer for you to spend the night again."

"Oh, thank you. You're so kind, but I need to get some of my belongings from home. We were just talking about the B and B. I'll probably stay there."

Abigail and Blake stayed and chatted for a few minutes. Darcy thought they paid particular attention to her, probably trying to get a feel for whether or not she could drive. She must have passed the test, because they took their leave and said they hoped to see her soon at the hospital when she comes to visit Jesse. Darcy liked that it didn't seem like a goodbye. Even though she knew that once she called Agent Danvers back, it very well could be.

Thomas turned to her as soon as the couple had left. "If you're ready, I'm ready."

Darcy nodded. "Then let's get going."

Thomas followed her out to the car.

"Would you like to drive?" she offered.

"I can't."

"Sure you can. You'll like it," she said. "It's a zippy little thing."

"No. Really, I can't. I don't have a license."

"Oh." Darcy climbed into the driver's seat. He scooted in beside her on the passenger side. He was so big he filled in the whole space. He carried Jesse's Bible.

"I thought we'd finally take it to the hospital to read to Jesse."

"Good idea." She took it from his hands and placed it behind the seat with her other things. "I've been thinking about what you said."

He lifted his shoulders. "About what?"

"About Jesse giving me information," she explained. "I was thinking when I get home I'll grab the letters Jesse wrote to me. I figure it can't hurt to look at them again. Right?"

"*Ja.* You should. But, Darcy, you don't plan to stay there, do you?"

"At my town house? No. Not after being attacked. Your grandmother is right that it would be easy for them to figure out where I live. I like the idea of the bed-and-breakfast. You think they'll have a room available?"

"One way to find out."

Darcy called as they drove out toward the highway and made a reservation.

After that, the drive seemed to go by in a blur. Darcy was tired and her head ached. It was a relief to arrive at their destination. She parked right in front of the town house. It seemed unusually dark. She exhaled slowly. *Home. Finally.*

She collected her purse and started to climb out of the car. "You coming?" she asked Thomas.

Thomas lifted his flip phone from his pocket, which had just started ringing. "I'll be right there."

She gathered up her things from the backseat and made her way up the narrow walk. She clutched at her unzipped coat as the wind whipped through the town house complex. Stepping onto her stoop, she held out her keys to unlock the front door. It was so dark, she could barely see to insert the key into the lock. Squinting at the doorknob, she stumbled forward. Her shoulder brushed against the door and it swung wide open.

Darcy gasped. She straightened herself and grabbed onto the door frame for balance, but she slipped. Her head pounded, as did her pulse. Never in a million years would she have left her town house unlocked. Someone had been inside her home.

"Hi. I was hoping to hear from you," Thomas said into his old flip phone as Darcy walked up to the front of her town house.

"I just heard from my friend at the Bureau, Agent Ross," Elijah said.

"Anything helpful?"

"I think so… Agent Ross was able to get access to sealed courtroom records. He found out that the man who testified against Wissenberg was named Michael Finlay. And he was a curator at the Gregorian Museum in Washington."

"Now that we know Jesse's real name," Thomas said, "does that help us know what these people are after?"

"To a certain extent. Wissenberg had a huge operation going. He stole art from private collectors around the world. Being the director of such a prestigious museum, he would easily get invitations into people's homes. His team would study and copy the works. In many cases, they bribed the owners' own cleaning staff or housekeepers to replace the original for the copies. It was sometimes months before an owner would realize he'd been robbed. Plus, Wissenberg took his time. He'd sometimes wait a year before executing a theft. It took a private art-insurance company doing years of legwork to even have a clue about what was happening, or how it was all connected. Wissenberg was so well-known and his work at the museum was so well respected that no one could believe it at first."

"Do you know how Jesse played into it?"

"Yes, in addition to working as curator, he was a talented artist himself—and he knew plenty of other painters willing to create forgeries for the right price. He recruited the team of artists who often made the reproductions. Very good reproductions," Elijah explained.

"Do you think Jesse knew what his artists were doing?" Thomas dropped his head into his hands.

"He knew about the forgeries, but I don't believe he was willing to be complicit in anything more physically harmful. After Wissenberg shot that night guard right in front of him, Jesse went to the authorities and agreed to testify against him. Jesse admitted to his own role in the fraud and thefts, but charges were dropped in exchange for his testimony. Reports indicate that Wissenberg possibly threatened him. The day before the trial, he and his wife were in a suspicious car accident. Margaret Finlay was killed instantly, although it's more likely that Michael— Jesse—was the real target."

"To keep him from testifying," Thomas said.

"Yes."

"But he testified anyway. And now Wissenberg is after him for revenge," Thomas said, still trying to make sense of it all. "But how does that explain the threats?"

"That's where it gets more complicated," Elijah admitted. "Apparently the system was that Wissenberg would pick the targets, commission the forgeries and then resell the originals, but the actual theft was handled by Jesse, working with whomever they had bribed inside the house. He'd take the frame off the original painting and replace it on the fake, then rehang it—he was the one with the experience and training to make the swap virtually undetectable. And then later, he'd turn the original paintings over to Wissenberg to resell. Wissenberg was the type to want to keep his hands clean—he was never actually there for the theft itself…except for one time."

"The night he shot the security guard," Thomas said, realizing what had happened.

"That's right. Apparently, it was a special commission— he had a buyer lined up who didn't want to wait. So Wissenberg went along so that he could deliver the painting directly to his buyer afterward. He wasn't as used to slipping in unnoticed as Jesse, though, and the security guard caught them. You know what happened from there."

"But what does that have to do with the threats?" Thomas asked again.

"The authorities were able to track most of the trafficked paintings, but Ross also found out that quite a few of the stolen originals were never recovered. There was some suspicion that Jesse had them, and never gave them to Wissenberg or the authorities."

"So Wissenberg thinks Jesse still has them." Thomas closed his eyes. "How much artwork are we talking about?"

"Ten million dollars' worth."

Thomas shook his head. He was about to reply when he heard a scream come from the still-dark town house. *Darcy!*

TEN

"Elijah, I'll call you back."

Thomas folded himself out of the small car and tossed his phone onto the seat as he raced to the town house's entrance. "Darcy? Are you okay?"

The front door was wide open and inside was nothing but darkness. Thomas stumbled over the threshold. "Darcy?"

A scuffling of feet sounded from the back of the home and then there was silence. Thomas lunged forward, tripping over a mass in the middle of the floor. When he heard the whimpering noise below him, he realized it was Darcy. He spread his arms out over her to keep from landing on top of her.

"Someone's here," she whispered.

"I think they just left. Are you okay?"

"Yes, I was just knocked down." Her voice sounded weak.

"Where's the light switch?"

"It wasn't working when I came in. They might have flipped the breakers, which are in the kitchen. All the way to the back," she said. "Take my phone. It has a flashlight."

Thomas groped around for her bag. "This is your bag, but it's empty."

"I guess whoever was here dumped it all out. Took something and ran."

Thomas felt around the floor and finally wrapped his hands around her fancy smartphone. "How do I—"

"Swipe up," she told him.

The bright flashlight illuminated the small entryway. Using its light, Thomas first checked Darcy. He slid his free arm under her shoulder and lifted her from the floor. She clung to him. He wanted to pull her tighter and take away all her pain and fear. He was starting now to understand her anger. She hadn't asked for any of this. She hadn't done anything to bring this threat to her doorstep. And yet, here was this horrible danger. And it was sounding more and more like Jesse was to blame for it.

"Here. Let's get you to a more comfortable place," he said.

"There's a couch. This way," she said, directing him.

He placed her down gently. "Whoever was here is gone now. But I'm sorry I didn't walk in with you—"

"Don't be," she interrupted. "You were here when I needed you. That's what matters."

When she looked up at him with eyes of thankfulness, his heart melted. She was so beautiful. So strong and yet so vulnerable. He tore his eyes away. "I'll go get that breaker."

He followed her directions to the kitchen, making his way around strangely placed items and furniture. He flipped the switch and the home lit up with soft lighting throughout, revealing a scene of absolute devastation. Ransacked. He made his way back to Darcy, who was already tearing up. "I'm calling the police now."

Darcy pulled herself up to a sitting position and swung her legs back around to the floor. Her home looked like a wreckage site. Chairs had been toppled over, drawers opened and emptied on the floor, the contents of closets strewn about. She could barely process it all. Thankfully, Thomas had known what to do. He had called the police and was talking to them now. He'd also called Elijah, who was on his way.

"Did you see who did this?" one of the officers asked Thomas.

"No. I could hear the intruder leaving by the time I came in."

"And you, Miss Simmons? Can you describe the intruder?"

Darcy shook her head. "No. He was behind me and it was very dark. But it didn't seem like he was alone. I think one of them had a gun to my neck."

"And they left through the back door?"

"Yes."

Darcy was growing tired. It was exhausting to have to answer questions about everything all over again. Thomas tried to intercept as many of the questions as he could. She was thankful for that.

"Miss Simmons, we are almost finished here, but since you've been part of the witness relocation program, you'll have to wait for an agent from the US Marshals to arrive. They'll take care of you."

Darcy swallowed hard. She didn't want to be taken care of. It seemed like the words were hardly out of the officer's mouth before Agent Danvers was standing at her door.

Just like at the hospital, she came blustering in, taking over the questioning and ordering the local authorities around. Darcy almost felt sorry for them except that at least the agent's attention was focused on them and what they were doing in her home, instead of on badgering or pressuring her.

"Elijah should be here soon. Blake is bringing him,"

Thomas whispered to her. "They will take us back to Willow Trace."

"You think their offer to stay at the clinic still stands?" She looked over at him. What would she have done through all of this without him?

"For sure." Nodding, he smiled and the warmth in his expression spread all the way to her own lips, which she felt curl up into a grin.

She reached over and touched her hand to his. "Thank you. Thank you for all you've done. You and all of your friends."

"The police are wondering what has been taken from your house. They want you to look around but I told them you couldn't."

"Darcy," Agent Danvers said as she came up behind them. "Did your father give you anything? Did he tell you about your past or about his past? Did he ask you to do anything for him?"

"You've already asked her that." Thomas stood and turned to face her.

Danvers took a step back. Darcy didn't blame her. Thomas was physically intimidating, even to someone as tall and fit as she was.

"Mr. Nolt, I appreciate your…help. But I am going to need to get Miss Simmons to a secure facility."

A secure facility? Darcy had been scared before, but it was nothing compared to the panic that rushed through her now. *What is this lady saying? A new identity?* Not yet. She wasn't ready for that. Darcy dropped her head between her hands. The pain seemed to triple. "Right now? I thought I had more time."

"Miss Simmons, surely this proves that you're not safe. You need to leave with me. The sooner the better. I was trying to give you more time, but…well, it's clearly too dangerous."

"You don't have to go with her," Thomas whispered to Darcy.

Darcy shut her eyes tight. If she could have, she would have willed herself to disappear off the sofa and escape all of this. But wasn't that what Agent Danvers was offering? So why not just go with her?

Thomas was glad to see Elijah and Blake pulling up behind the police cars in the complex's parking lot. He hoped they could help convince Darcy not to go with Agent Danvers. Not now that they knew what Wissenberg was after. There was hope that they could get this figured out and everyone would be safe. Both Jesse and Darcy. Without anyone needing to start his or her life over. At least, it was worth a try. Maybe they needed to search Jesse's cottage again. Maybe they needed to look at the letters Jesse had sent Darcy. But there were clues to follow—things they could do. He didn't want her to go. What would he tell Jesse when he woke up if he had let his friend's daughter walk away forever?

Thomas hated seeing Darcy struggle so with the decision. He supposed Danvers was doing her job, but she was such a bully. And he was certain that Blake and Abigail could keep Darcy safe for at least one more night. Thomas filled in his friends on what had happened and why Danvers was there.

"Well, I know how to put a stop to that," said Blake. He stepped away and headed straight to the US Marshal.

"She's in shock," Blake declared. "You can't expect her to make a life-altering decision like this in her condition."

"This is exactly how these decisions are made," the

agent insisted. "If everything was all hunky-dory they wouldn't need to be in the program."

"She has a head injury and is under my care," said Blake. "I will not release her over to any agency until she's had further treatment and an exam."

If Blake was bluffing, Thomas thought, he was doing a pretty good job of it. Thomas hoped it would work. He at least wanted to have the chance to tell her what Elijah had learned. She would want to know.

"And you are?" Agent Danvers lifted an eyebrow.

"Dr. Jamison, head of ER at Lancaster General," Blake said.

"I thought Miss Simmons was released yesterday after I met with her," she said.

"That is correct. However, we are waiting for some of the swelling to go down before doing a second exam," Blake said.

"So you're taking her back to Lancaster?"

"Yes," said Blake.

Danvers sighed and dropped her arms to her sides. She turned to Darcy. "Then I'll expect a call from you as soon as this exam is over. I'll pick you up at the hospital."

Darcy did not respond. She actually did look like she was in shock. Perhaps Blake's words had been the truth.

Danvers took her leave in a mad rush. Her frustration seemed to be oozing from her hard glare at Thomas and his friends as she walked out. Thomas was not sorry she was leaving alone. Darcy didn't belong with her. That he was sure of.

"I'm glad you got here when you did," Darcy said. "Maybe I should go with her, but—"

"No. You shouldn't. Not today, at least," Elijah said.

"You have a better idea?" she asked, lifting a hand to her head.

Thomas smiled. His friend Elijah always had a better idea.

"Okay. Okay," Blake said. "Clearly there are things we all need to discuss. But first let's get Darcy some fluids. And by the looks of it, some pain meds."

The medication Blake administered started to take the edge off her pain. Darcy was able to stand and gather a few personal belongings. She was so thankful she had stayed behind. Saved once again by her three musketeers of Willow Trace. They had even straightened up her town house a little. And she'd learned what Wissenberg was after and why. She even knew Jesse's former name now. Finlay. Michael Finlay. And her mother had been Margaret Finlay. That would have been her last name, too. Not Simmons. She wondered what her own first name had been.

"Do you think anything is missing?" Thomas queried as he walked into her room. "I know you've been asked that a million times tonight, but Elijah says it's really important and I figured maybe now you've had a chance to look around."

"It's a mess, but I don't really notice that anything is gone. Certainly not any of the things a thief would usually target, like my computer or TV." Darcy blinked and concentrated on his question. "But you're asking about the things that Jesse gave me?"

He shrugged. "You were going to look for the letters."

"Right." She reached around her neck. The locket was still there. "The letters would be in the front hall. I kept them in a basket."

He followed her to the foyer. The basket had been toppled. Some of its contents were on the floor. But no letters. Darcy crouched and looked around.

"Allow me." Thomas swept the floor with his big arms.

He pulled up a few bills, some junk mail and a magazine. But none of Jesse's letters.

She opened the drawer to the console table. Empty.

"They're gone. All of the letters Jesse wrote to me are gone."

ELEVEN

Darcy slept all the way back to Lancaster County. Thomas was glad for that. After what she'd been through, she deserved the chance to rest a bit, surrounded by people who made her feel safe. He only hoped they wouldn't let her down.

Elijah was on and off the phone, talking to McClendon and to his agent friend at the FBI. The more Thomas overheard the conversations, the more he worried.

Elijah had suggested that Darcy leave both her phone and her car behind. There could be a tracking device on the car, to say nothing of the ways to trace an unencrypted phone. Darcy had readily agreed. Thomas had her cancel her reservation at the Willow Trace Bed-and-Breakfast. For this night, she would sleep again at the clinic. Blake truly did want to reexamine her head injury in the morning. It was a needed precaution after she'd fallen again. But after that, what would or should they do?

"Where are we?" she said, half waking up.

"Almost to the clinic," Thomas said.

Abigail came out to Blake's truck and helped to escort Darcy back to the guest room.

"She's changing," Abigail said, returning to the kitchen, where Thomas, Elijah and Blake sat discussing the evening.

"I'm glad she's safe," Thomas said.

"She wanted to know if she could visit Jesse tomorrow. I didn't know what to tell her," Abigail said.

"I don't know if she should go anywhere," Elijah said. "At least, not as Darcy Simmons."

"You think she should go with Agent Danvers, take on a new identity somewhere else?" Thomas felt his blood pressure rise. How could Elijah suggest such a thing?

"No. I don't," Elijah said.

That was a relief, Thomas thought. "So your solution is just to keep her inside until all of this is over?"

"No, I don't even know if that would be enough," Elijah admitted. "If Wissenberg was able to find Jesse and Darcy once, what's to stop him from finding her again? Staying home wasn't enough to protect Jesse."

"So, you have a better idea?" Abigail lifted her eyebrows at her brother.

Elijah grinned. "Of course I do. But I don't know if Darcy will agree to it."

"You want me to do what?" Darcy could feel her eyes practically popping out of their sockets. It seemed Elijah had come up with an interesting idea to keep her safe while she had been changing her clothes. He was now sharing the plan with all of them as they sat around Abigail's kitchen table. Darcy, stunned, had had to ask him to repeat it again.

"It's called hiding in plain sight," Elijah explained. "It's just for a few days."

"No. I can't do that," Darcy shook her head. She could not—would not—do what they were asking. "I've already depended on you way more than is fair to you. It's not your job to keep protecting me."

"Well, we kind of think it is," Thomas said. "It is for Jesse. You're his daughter after all."

"I don't know." Darcy tried to come up with a good alternative plan. But what could she do? Call Danvers? Stay with a friend in town and put them in danger? Stay in a hotel? Run away?

She didn't like any of those options, either.

"Do you really think it will hide me? These people know what I look like," she said. "They got a pretty good look at me at Jesse's yesterday."

"Yes, but in your *Englisch* clothes. In those you're pretty easy to identify. If you dress Amish, you will blend in with us. From a distance or in a crowd of other Amish, you'll be pretty tough to spot. They won't be looking for you in a frock. And like I said, it's just for a few days."

"What's going to change in a few days?"

"Hopefully Jesse will wake up," said Thomas. "And while we are waiting, we are going to comb through Jesse's cottage and find any and every clue we can. There could be something in his cottage from his past. Something besides pictures."

Darcy didn't like the idea of dressing Amish and staying with Elijah and Hannah, putting them in danger. In fact, she hated the idea. But she did not have a better one, and she could see the logic in the decision. Elijah was a former policeman, able to take care of himself and trained in providing protection. Hannah was aware of the danger and had agreed to this. Hiding with the Amish would let her stay close to Jesse and help search for answers while keeping her hidden.

"Okay, then," Darcy said. "I hope you're good at makeovers."

"I can't do this." Darcy leaned into Abigail's mirror. "Look at me. I look ridiculous. I *feel* ridiculous."

After a morning shower, Abigail had helped Darcy get into her Amish costume—blouse, frock and *kapp*. Her bandage was gone and with her hair parted straight down the middle, the stitches were barely visible.

Abigail smiled at her. "Actually, you make me a little homesick. I mean I didn't really leave home, but when I made the choice not to be baptized, I left that lifestyle behind. But before that, I'd dressed like that my whole life. You look like home to me. I think you look beautiful."

Darcy looked to Abigail with an apologetic frown. "I'm sorry. I didn't mean to—"

"No, no, no." Abigail walked over to her and tied her *kapp* in a loose bow, leaving the straps to hang to her chest.

She looked again at herself in the mirror. They were right. She would be hard to recognize. She wasn't even sure she recognized herself. "It feels like a costume."

"I understand. It's not what you're used to. But trust me, you look just fine. And this will keep you safe until my brother and Thomas work this all out."

"You sound pretty confident in their abilities." Darcy wanted to believe her, but she had little hope. "You really think they can solve a mystery that has endured over two decades?"

"Anyone can if they look in the right places. There are always signs around us that lead to the truth."

"I hope you're right," Darcy said. "Okay, tell me what to do. What do I say when people talk to me?"

"Just be yourself. Remember, we are not people who ask a lot of questions."

"Right."

"And be useful, wherever you can," Abigail advised.

"But I can't cook. I know nothing about horses and farms. And I really know nothing about God."

Darcy knew she had just a few minutes before it was time to go to the Millers'.

Why was she so nervous? Everyone was there to help her through this. Still, she could feel her heart pounding and her palms sweating.

What if her presence brought harm to these good people? What if Jesse didn't wake up? What if she never discovered the truth and she would have to leave and start her life anew?

"God loves you, as He loves all of us. And when we do His will, we know Him. This will be a good time for you, Darcy. I am sure of it. We should go now."

Darcy closed her eyes. How was she going to get through this?

Abigail put her arm around Darcy's shoulder and began to lead her toward the front of the clinic. It was time to go.

"Don't worry. All will be well, Darcy."

At the designated time, Thomas drove his horse and buggy over to the clinic to pick up the Millers' new house-guest. Thomas had offered to pick her up since it seemed everyone else was busy. Elijah had business with his father. The women were all excited to show off their great cooking to Darcy. Nana had even gotten up early and headed to the market with the bishop's wife in order to get extra provisions for the evening meal. Thomas was glad that he and Nana had been invited to dinner, too. He wanted to keep an eye on Darcy as much as possible. He was very glad she'd decided to accept Elijah's plan and he was happy to drive her to the Millers'.

Thomas pulled Sadie up in front of the clinic and hitched her to the post. He paced across the front porch, sweating slightly despite the cold winter air. The morning sun peeked occasionally through a fluffy band of clouds headed north and east. The year's first snowfall would be upon them soon.

When Abigail appeared at the front door, Thomas wiped his palms against the front of his trousers. Darcy was standing behind her wearing one of Abigail's old dresses.

"I know," Darcy said. "I look so—so…"

"Plain." Thomas was careful not to stare but it was hard. It was strange to see her in plain clothing. He could only imagine how strange it must have felt to her.

"She worked on it all morning," Abigail said. "My clothes were way too big for her. She's pretty handy with a needle and thread."

"So I've already heard," Thomas said, daring to look up again at Darcy. She wore a dark gray frock that accented the color of her big eyes. Over the dress was a neatly pressed black apron. On her feet she wore a pair of old leather lace-up boots.

She laughed and pointed to her head. "I don't think I've parted my hair down the middle since I was in the first grade."

She hardly looked like a first grader, Thomas thought. "It suits you. Not a trace of *Englisch* about you now."

Darcy looked desperately to Abigail. "What? What does that mean?"

"*Englisch* are what the Amish call everyone who's not Amish." Abigail showed Thomas to Darcy's bag before giving Darcy a reassuring hug. "Just relax and enjoy your time with the Millers."

Darcy flushed. The creaminess of her complexion highlighted her dark eyes and high cheekbones more than any store-bought makeup could have. He swallowed hard and looked away, while Darcy thanked Abigail for her help.

"Remember, Thomas, she still needs to take it easy,"

Abigail said, then looked to Darcy. "If you get the least bit dizzy, stop what you're doing and give me a call."

Darcy nodded.

Abigail gave her one more reassuring glance then waved goodbye from the front porch.

"Well, then," he said. "I suppose we should get going. Hannah is anxious to see you."

She followed him out to the vehicle. He gave her a hand into the front seat. "My first time in a horse-drawn buggy."

"It's a little chilly today," he noted as he untied Sadie and climbed into the driver's seat. "You're gonna want this blanket." He reached into the back and handed her the thick wool coverlet that he kept there for the cold days.

He gave Sadie a tap with the reins and the mare took off onto the highway. Darcy was quiet at first, fidgeting with her hands. Then she tucked the blanket around herself tighter.

"You weren't kidding," she said as she shivered. "It's cold."

Thomas passed the reins to her. "Here. Take them."

"What? I don't—"

"One second. Just hold them."

Reluctantly, she took the long leather straps into her hands.

Thomas waited another second, then he took off his coat and placed it around Darcy's shoulders.

He wasn't sure, but he thought he saw a few tears in her eyes.

"Thank you. Thank you for everything you're doing for me."

Thomas took the reins back into his left hand. Then he took his right arm and placed it around Darcy's torso. He pulled her next to him on the bench.

"This way I can stay warm, too," he said, but that wasn't the only reason he wanted her close.

Darcy was the one to protect, but Thomas knew if he wasn't careful with his heart, he was going to be in more danger than Darcy. Just a different sort of danger.

TWELVE

It was a whole other perspective of the Amish countryside, seeing it from inside Thomas's buggy. The *clippity-clop* of the horse's beat. The cold air. The smell of the outdoors, fresh and wild and clean. And Thomas, so close beside her. Darcy watched him tap the reins on the back of his horse. "What's he like?"

"Who? Jesse?" Thomas asked.

"Yes, I mean more like what does he do? What did he do for a living?" she said.

"Well, when he first came here, he secured a job at Millers' Furniture immediately."

"As in Elijah Miller?"

"His father, the bishop, owns an Amish furniture-making business."

"What did Jesse do there?"

"He made and designed furniture."

Darcy swallowed hard. Her father was so interesting and it was fascinating to discover that she shared some of his interests. She loved art and design. *He* loved art and design. Maybe it was a silly thing to cling to. But she'd lived her whole life knowing nothing, so now every little thing she heard, she couldn't help but try to relate to herself in some way.

"Yes. He was really good at it. He made all of the furniture in his cottage," Thomas said.

"It's beautiful. He must have done well."

"He did but he quit and went to work for my father after a while," Thomas said.

"Why?"

"He got a little too creative. He varied too much from the traditional Amish style. Too much detail. Too fancy. So Bishop Miller couldn't sell what he made in his store. Jesse considered selling through other vendors, but being a part of the community was more important to him than his gifts and skill with wood. So he apprenticed as a farrier with my father and he became one of the best in the county."

"My dad worked with horses?"

"Yes, still does. He stays busy, too. All the Amish buggy horses have shoes."

"It's a shame about the letters," she said.

"Well, at least you still have your locket."

"Yes, Abigail said it would be okay to wear it as long as I keep it under the dress."

He nodded. "You know… Jesse's going to wake up."

"How do you know?" He seemed so sure.

"I don't. I just hope and I pray."

"And God answers your prayers?"

"Always. It's not always the answer I was hoping for. Sometimes it's even better." Thomas cleared his throat. "Do you think there was anything in the letters that could be useful? Can you remember?"

"I don't think so." Darcy thought hard, trying to remember the contents. "But I was so overwhelmed by the whole idea of having a father who was alive that I might have missed something."

Thomas took off his hat and ran his hand through his

dark curls. "I have a hard time believing that Jesse would have done anything purposely to put you in harm's way. Most likely, he had no idea that Wissenberg was going to get out of prison so soon."

"Do you think it's possible that Jesse really has millions of dollars' worth of stolen artwork hidden away somewhere?"

"I don't want to believe it," Thomas said. "But all these attacks would seem to prove that Wissenberg is convinced."

Darcy hated that. She hated thinking that her dad was a selfish crook, hiding away art instead of returning it to the rightful owners.

"Do you think it's worth going back over to the cottage to see if anything is there that the police didn't find?"

"I don't know. Maybe." Thomas looked up. "That's the Miller house up ahead."

A gray farmhouse came into view. Unlike Thomas's home, the stable was a long distance from the house and much smaller. Hannah met her at the door holding a six-to nine-month-old baby boy in her arms.

"Where was this fellow the other day?" Darcy asked.

"With my mother-in-law," Hannah said. "Please come in and let me show you to your room. I've been instructed that you need a lot of rest."

Darcy nodded. She had to admit she was tired. She said goodbye to Thomas and followed Hannah through the house. It was an old place, with low ceilings and tiny rooms. "This house must have been built before the Civil War."

"Before the Revolutionary War." Hannah laughed. "It's been in the Miller family for a long time."

"It's charming," Darcy said. And it was, in its own way.

The Miller family had done well to preserve the old wood and trim. And it was surprisingly warm.

"You'll be in here." Hannah showed her a small bedroom that had little more in it than a single bed, a wooden table with a lantern and a chair. "Please rest up and I'll call you for lunch."

Darcy went inside. Hannah closed the door behind her. As grateful as she was for a safe place to stay, a big part of her wanted to put her own clothes back on and reclaim her life. But that wasn't an option just now, so she gave in to her other temptation. She lay down and slept.

Thomas hoped Darcy would get some rest. He knew Hannah would take good care of her, as would Elijah and the bishop. So why did he not like leaving? He would be back for dinner, he reminded himself.

As Sadie trotted thought the forest, Thomas couldn't help but think about the drive over to the Millers'. In fact, he thought over everything that had transpired recently. To think that it was just several days ago when he was riding to Jesse's to take a look at his well. It seemed like decades had passed.

Jesse's well. Come to think of it, he never had taken a look at it. He would have to do that before Jesse came back home from the hospital. Just thinking of Jesse filled Thomas with a powerful urge to see his friend. Thomas had chores to do but nothing that couldn't wait. Instead of driving Sadie back home, he went to the hospital and sat with Jesse. He'd been there for a few minutes when the quiet was interrupted by a voice from the doorway.

"So where is she?"

Thomas turned around to find Agent Danvers. She was wearing the same dark US Marshals coat and sporting the same spiky hairdo. "Where is who? Miss Simmons?"

"Yes, Miss Simmons." The agent crossed her arms over her chest and widened her stance. "Who else?"

"Why would you think I might know where Miss Simmons is?" He turned his back to her and looked down at Jesse, lying there helpless in the hospital bed.

"The two of you have seemed inseparable," Danvers snarled.

"She's not with me now," Thomas answered.

"I know you know where she is," Danvers accused as she stepped into the room.

Thomas struggled to control his temper. He really didn't like this woman. "I do know where she is. And I know that she is safe. That's all you need to know, as well."

Thomas stood. He turned around and headed out of the small room, forcing the agent to move backward.

"I'll just follow you," she said, as he walked past.

"It's a free country," Thomas replied over his shoulder as he walked on.

"You can't keep her safe, farmer boy," she yelled after him.

Turn the other cheek. Turn the other cheek, Thomas repeated in his mind. Danvers's behavior had crossed the line. But he walked on in silence. In a way, he hoped she did follow him. He was headed straight to Jesse's cottage and if she trailed him there, he would call Chief McClendon and whoever else he needed to put an end to her bullying.

Still, as he left the hospital, her words rang over and over through his head. Mostly because he feared that she was right.

He couldn't keep her safe. He was just a farmer.

Thomas drove his buggy down the highway, more determined than ever to help Darcy and Jesse. He reached for his phone.

"How is she?" he asked Elijah.

"She's been sleeping all day," his friend said. "Hannah's been checking on her regularly. She took her some stew for lunch. She's fine."

"I saw Danvers at the hospital. She threatened to follow me. She wants Darcy."

Elijah was silent for a moment. "Where are you now?"

"I'm heading home, but I'm going to stop by Uncle Jesse's first. It looks like snow and I just want to at least turn off his water so that he doesn't come home to a burst pipe."

"I'll meet you there. You shouldn't go there alone."

"I'll be fine. You stay with Darcy. I'll see you at dinner."

Thomas felt exposed as he pulled up to Jesse's cottage. But he reminded himself that Darcy was safely tucked away at the Millers' and that he was just there to turn off the water and take a peek at the well.

He parked his buggy at the house. As the wind whipped across the open hills, Thomas pulled his coat collar up around his neck. It was definitely going to freeze tonight. He walked around to the back of the building, removed the side panel, which led to under the house, reached in and turned off the main.

Sadie whinnied and snorted at the front of the house. Was someone there? Thomas's thoughts flashed back to the past few days. Maybe Elijah was right. He shouldn't have come there alone.

No. Thomas shook away his fear. *If the Lord is for us then who can be against us? Romans 8:31*

Thomas scanned the fields. He saw nothing but he distinctly felt as if someone was nearby. Someone was watching him. Had Agent Danvers really followed him? Or was he just being paranoid?

He headed to the well. He slid off the lid and looked down inside. Everything seemed to be in order. Thomas was ready to slide the lid back over when his eyes spotted a little box attached to the inside wall.

What was that?

Thomas reached inside and unhitched the box. He tried to open it but the little box was locked. Thomas took it back to the buggy and headed home. Whatever was in the little chest was sealed up tight. Maybe he could open it later with tools.

Was this what Jesse had called him over for? Did Jesse know it was there? Did it have anything to do with Wissenberg and the missing art?

Thomas didn't know, but as the buggy entered the woods, he was sure that someone was watching him.

FREE Merchandise is 'in the Cards' for you!

Dear Reader,

We're giving away FREE MERCHANDISE!

Seriously, we'd like to reward you for reading this novel by giving you **FREE MERCHANDISE** worth over $20 retail. And no purchase is necessary!

You see the Jack of Hearts sticker above? Paste that sticker in the box on the Free Merchandise Voucher inside. Return the Voucher today... and we'll send you Free Merchandise!

Thanks again for reading one of our novels—and enjoy your Free Merchandise with our compliments!

Pam Powers

Pam Powers

P.S. Look inside to see what Free Merchandise is **"in the cards"** for you!

We'd like to send you two free books like the one you are enjoying now. Your two books have a combined cover price of over $10 retail, but they are yours to keep absolutely FREE! We'll even send you 2 wonderful surprise gifts. You can't lose!

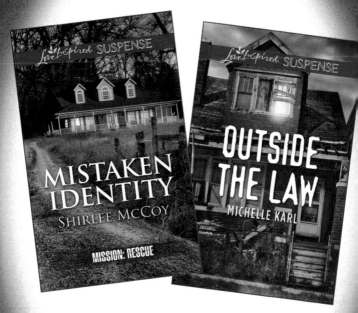

REMEMBER: Your Free Merchandise, consisting of **2 Free Books** and **2 Free Gifts**, is worth over $20 retail! No purchase is necessary, so please send for your Free Merchandise today.

Get TWO FREE GIFTS!

We'll also send you 2 wonderful FREE GIFTS (worth about $10 retail), in addition to your 2 Free books!

Visit us at:
www.ReaderService.com

Books received may not be as shown.

FREE MERCHANDISE VOUCHER

2 FREE
BOOKS
and
2 FREE
GIFTS

Please send my Free Merchandise, consisting of
2 Free Books and **2 Free Mystery Gifts**.
I understand that I am under no obligation to buy
anything, as explained on the back of this card.

❏ I prefer the regular-print edition   ❏ I prefer the larger-print edition
153/353 IDL GLTN   107/307 IDL GLTN

Please Print

FIRST NAME

LAST NAME

ADDRESS

APT.#

CITY

STATE/PROV.

ZIP/POSTAL CODE

NO PURCHASE NECESSARY!

SLI-517-FM17

THIRTEEN

"Darcy?"

There was knocking. Someone was at the door. But Darcy could barely focus. Her head was clouded with sleep.

"Darcy? Time for supper. Everyone is here."

What? Supper?

The voice had an accent that was both strange and familiar. Where was she? Darcy blinked her eyes open. She was enveloped in darkness. What time was is? She sat up. This was not her bed.

"Darcy? Are you awake?"

It was Hannah. She was at the Millers' home. In the middle of Amish country. Dressed like she was Amish. She put a hand to her head. Her hair was still pulled tight at the base of her neck.

"Yes, I'm awake. Barely." She swung her feet around to the floor.

"Let me come in and light the lantern for you," Hannah offered.

The auburn-haired Amish woman floated across the old wooden floor and grabbed something off the table. Soon the tiny room filled with a soft yellow glow.

"To the left is the bathroom," she said. "If you'd like to wash up before dinner."

She turned back to the door but paused before leaving. "Darcy? Are you okay?"

Was she okay?

"I'm fine. I'm just a little disoriented," Darcy said. "You know how it is after a deep sleep."

Hannah nodded. "Thomas is here. He has something for you."

Darcy rubbed her eyes, still foggy from sleep. Thomas. She'd dreamed of him—of his brown eyes and his wide smile. She'd dreamed of his soft, deep voice and the weight of his arm around her shoulder. *He had something for her?*

Darcy shook her head. She was awake now and remembering everything that had happened over the past few days. She hoped whatever Thomas had was what they needed to end all of this, so that she could go home. She needed to get out of here. Back to her life. Back into her clothes. And away from Thomas and his big brown eyes. Thomas could never be interested in someone *Englisch*. And she shouldn't be interested in someone Amish. She didn't even know how to pray. How could she fall for a person whose whole life revolved around faith? How could that ever work?

It couldn't.

"It was in Jesse's well." Thomas handed the small wooden box to Darcy. He had stayed behind with her in the Millers' kitchen so that he could give it to her without so many others around. He had no idea what was inside. Maybe nothing of importance. But the more he had thought about it, the more Thomas had decided that it might not have been a coincidence that Jesse had asked him to come over "to look at the well" at the same time as he'd been expecting Darcy.

Then again, he was probably just overthinking it all in the hope that he would find answers.

"It's a nice box." She took it from his hands. "You found it inside Jesse's well?"

"*Ja.* I just went by there to turn off the water so the pipes don't freeze tonight and I remembered that the day I met you, he had asked me to come look at the well. So I thought I might as well have a look at it. And I found this."

"It looks handmade." She turned the box over in her hands, touching the complicated pattern of inlays.

"I'm sure Jesse made it."

"It's beautiful, but why did you bring it to me?"

Why had he brought it to her? Thomas felt heat rise to his cheeks. "I started to open it at home with tools, but I knew that might ruin it. And I wanted you to see it before that, since we had been talking about his craftsmanship."

But that wasn't the only reason why he'd waited. It had also been an excuse to spend a moment with Darcy. An excuse to speak with her again. "Plus, it just seemed wrong to open it up without you."

"Speaking of opening it," she said. "How are we going to do that? It's locked up. Looks like it needs a key."

Thomas took the box back from her, his hand lingering maybe a moment too long as his fingers grazed over hers in the exchange.

"See these inlays?"

She nodded.

"These are the reason that Jesse's furniture could not be sold as Amish."

Thomas turned the box over in his hands, touching each one of the inlays. "Once Jesse told me that fancy things were just a way for the *Englisch* to hide the real truth in their life."

He used his fingernail to pry at each of the inlays. One of the pieces popped out with ease.

Darcy picked up the block of polished wood and turned it over. Inside was a tiny key.

"You do the honors, please," Thomas said.

"Okay." She smiled and placed the key delicately into the box lock. It opened on the first try. Slowly, Darcy lifted the lid.

"It's pictures. Old Polaroids."

Thomas put the box down on the table and held the lid back. Darcy reached in and pulled out the stack of photos.

"Oh, my," she said, turning through them one after the other. "They're pictures of paintings. Really nice paintings."

"There's something written on the back of each photo, too."

She flipped the pictures over one at a time. "Phelps. Thurston. Davies. Beauchamps. Geigenhaus…"

"Could those be the names of the artists?" Thomas mused.

"I don't know." She shook her head back and forth, her eyes wide with excitement. "But are you thinking what I'm thinking?"

Thomas nodded. "That this could be the missing art everyone is hoping to find…or at least pictures of it."

"Exactly!" Darcy stared up at him. "I don't know whether to be happy or sad at finding this."

Thomas wanted to hug her and comfort her through the disappointment she was feeling in finding yet another clue that shed more suspicion over Jesse. He felt it, too. "I think we can be thankful for more information. In any case, we don't know what these mean. Not yet anyway."

She nodded. "I guess we should call the police. Again."

* * *

After dinner, Chief McClendon and another man named Agent Frank Ross of the FBI sat with Thomas, Elijah and Darcy at the Millers' kitchen table. The FBI agent was a small man in his late forties, dressed informally in jeans, a T-shirt and a big blue jacket that said FBI in huge yellow letters. He looked at each of the pictures quickly then scanned them into a tiny handheld scanner, which was hooked up to his laptop.

After each photo he was able to quickly identify the painting. "This is *Sunny Day* by the artist Florence Ko. Stolen from Mrs. Deveraux of McClain, Virginia, twenty-five years ago. Never recovered."

"*Deveraux* is the name written on the back of the photo," Darcy said.

Elijah stood from the table and began to pace. "There are fifteen photos. Fifteen stolen paintings. None of them were ever recovered. Jesse clearly had them in his possession at one point, and kept a record of them all. But why?"

Thomas fidgeted with the empty box that had contained the photos. He hated how guilty all this made Jesse seem. Why had he had these paintings? Why had he kept pictures of them? And why had he asked him to come and look at the well? Jesse would have known that Thomas would have spotted the box. Jesse must have wanted him to find it or to retrieve it for him. But why?

The FBI agent pushed his equipment aside and cleared his throat. "The good news is that the statute of limitations would be in effect for all of this stolen property. So Jesse cannot be tried for possession of these, if indeed he does have the actual works. But honestly, there is no evidence of that here. It seems likely that he took these pictures a long time ago, and that the artwork was in his possession when he did so, but we can't know that for sure. It doesn't mean he has the paintings now. These photos don't prove anything except that Jesse knew whom the artwork was stolen from."

"And why would a thief care about that?" McClendon asked, his voice dripping with sarcasm.

Jesse was far more than just a thief, Thomas thought to himself. Thomas refused to believe that until the day that Jesse told him otherwise. Maybe he was blinded by his love for the old man. But better that than thinking so single-mindedly.

"He wanted to remember who the works belonged to," Thomas said. "You're right. I wouldn't think your everyday thief would care about knowing that. In fact, he'd probably want to forget whom he stole from. But Jesse wanted to remember, because…"

"Because he wanted to return them?" Darcy suggested hopefully.

Thomas looked across the table at her and smiled. She didn't want to think badly of her father, either.

"That's really irrelevant," Elijah said. "What we need to know is where Jesse put the actual paintings. Did he pass them on to another party? Maybe he sold them?"

"First thing tomorrow, I'm sending a small investigative team to Jesse's cottage," said Agent Ross.

"We've already had a team there," said McClendon.

"Yes, but they were investigating a break-in and a beating," said Elijah. "Agent Ross is right. We have a lot more information now. A new search will be much more focused."

"Could Elijah and I be there?" asked Thomas.

"Me, too?" said Darcy.

"Is that a good idea?" Thomas said. "I mean, is that safe?"

Agent Ross collected his things from the table. "I can't

think of a safer place for her to be than surrounded by a crew of FBI agents. Right?"

Right. But why did Thomas still feel like it was a bad idea? He kept his mouth closed. Darcy looked happier than she had all evening.

"Okay, see you bright and early tomorrow." Agent Ross took his leave.

McClendon followed.

Thomas called Nana and they, too, headed out into the night to make their way home.

Again, he felt as if someone was watching him.

You can't keep her safe, farmer boy.

FOURTEEN

The new search at Jesse's had turned up nothing. And to make matters worse, Blake had called with the news that Jesse's stats had taken a slight turn for the worse.

The Elders would soon have to decide how long they would keep Jesse on life support.

"What will happen to all of this beautiful furniture if Jesse…" Darcy looked around at the cottage and all the pieces inside it that her father had made.

Thomas swallowed hard. "If Jesse passes? Normally it would all be auctioned or go to families in need, but I suppose now it could all go to you. You'd have to speak with the Elders about that. They make those sorts of decisions. But, Darcy, Jesse may pull through yet. Have a little faith."

Elijah came into the room. "The FBI team is heading out. And I have to go, as well. My father called and he needs help with a delivery. Thomas, is Nana still hosting that barn singing tonight?"

"*Ja*. As far as I know," Thomas answered.

"Barn singing?" Darcy asked. "What's that?"

"It's a social meeting for the young folk," Thomas said to Darcy then turned to Elijah. "You're coming, aren't you?"

"Of course, I think my dad still has the buggy with all

the benches so we will be there early. Though that's a lot of buggy riding for Miss Simmons—riding all the way home with me now and then heading back this way later."

"Darcy can come spend the afternoon with us," Thomas offered. "Stay for the singing and ride home with you and Hannah? If that's okay with her?"

"Sure," she said.

Darcy was actually relieved. She liked the Millers and was more than grateful for their hospitality, but she felt like an imposition. She should probably feel that way about going to the Nolts' home, but with Thomas and Nana, it just didn't seem as awkward.

"Okay, then. We will see you later. I'm sorry this didn't pan out today, Darcy. But we just have to keep thinking." Elijah turned and was gone.

The house cleared out quickly, leaving Darcy and Thomas alone to close up.

"We should get going," Thomas said. "Nana is going to love having you over today. And there will be a lot to do to get ready for the singing."

"And what about you?" she asked. "I hope you don't mind my being there. Elijah didn't really leave you much of a choice."

Thomas grinned slightly, but he wouldn't look up to meet her eye. "You will always be welcome in my home, Darcy."

"Thank you but I don't think I'll be much help to either you or Nana. I don't sing."

Thomas burst out laughing. Darcy felt heat rise to her cheeks.

"We won't be singing," he said. "Only the youth. It's really more of a social thing. But there is lots of food to prepare. And a little extra work to do in the stable."

"Sounds like I can pitch in. And it is the least I can do

after all the help you and your friends have given me," she said.

"You know I'm really sorry we didn't find anything else here today," he said. "I just thought that if Jesse left those photographs behind then he probably left something else."

"You're right. We just have to stay focused." Darcy looked around the cottage at all of Jesse's belongings. Thomas had been right about the furniture designs not quite being suitable for the Amish. They were in the same style as the ones in his home and in the Millers' home, but the extra flourishes meant they did not exactly fit. All of the pieces had inlays like the box Thomas had found in the well. An idea occurred to her.

"Thomas, does the FBI know that Jesse used to make furniture?"

"I don't know," Thomas said. "I think I mentioned that he'd made that box I found the photos in. Why do you ask?"

"It's nothing really," Darcy said, but the idea she had kept coming back to her. "I guess I was wondering about the possibility that Jesse may have built something special into one of these pieces of furniture that he made."

"What do you mean? Like a hiding place? A secret compartment?"

"Yes, exactly. I did that once for a friend of mine who was getting married." Darcy smiled as she remembered the beautiful dress she had sewn for her friend. "She wanted a hidden pocket in her dress so that she could put her 'something blue' in it. It was this huge sapphire that had belonged in her family for years and she didn't want to worry about losing it on her big day. Anyway, I loved the idea. It was easy to do. In fact, after that dress, I ended up selling the idea to a large bridal dress manufacturer.

Now those 'something blue' pockets are sewn in a whole line of dresses."

"Sounds impressive," Thomas said.

"Thanks. But actually, my point is that maybe Jesse hid something in his furniture. Like the secret key in the inlay last night. Maybe there's another one in here?"

Thomas was nodding. "Won't hurt to look."

Both of them started running their hands over each piece of finely made wooden furniture, tugging at every joint and pressing on every fancy detail. They worked their way through all the downstairs furniture and found nothing.

"Might as well try the loft, too," Darcy said.

Thomas followed her up the narrow wooden steps. "You take the left. I'll take the right."

Darcy started with a small chair and a nightstand. Thomas went to what was probably the largest and most ornate piece in the whole house. But instead of running his hands over it, he took off his hat and turned it in his hands.

"It's this. It's the highboy," he said. "Come look."

"How do you know?" Darcy walked toward him. "You haven't even touched it."

"I should have thought of it before," he said. "Someone wanted to buy it from Miller's shop. It was a long time ago."

"Buy what? This highboy?"

"Yes, but Jesse wouldn't sell it. Bishop Miller was pretty put out with him. He said he shouldn't be building pieces at the shop that weren't actually for sale. I don't think they talked to each other for a week after that." He grinned at the memory.

Darcy ran her hands over the piece. She pried at the inlays but there weren't that many. This piece was hand carved and had amazing detail on the legs and feet. "Nothing's moving."

"Here, take a look at this." He leaned over and pointed. At the bottom of the highboy was a long piece of intricate trim, on either side of it a small drawer. "Why put a panel here instead of another drawer?"

"You think there's something behind the panel?"

Thomas shrugged. "I think it's worth checking."

He loped back down the stairs.

"Where are you going?"

"Jesse kept his carpentry tools down here. I don't want to just rip the panel off," he called from the stairs.

Thomas soon returned with a small wooden chisel and a soft cloth in his hands. He went back to the highboy. She moved out of his way and watched as he covered the tip of the tool with the cheesecloth so as not to damage the beautiful piece of furniture before prying open the panel. It took some maneuvering, but slowly, steadily, he worked the thick, decorative plank loose.

"Oh, my, Thomas, look. You were right. There's a secret shelf." Darcy felt her heart pumping hard.

Thomas reached in slowly then stopped, hand in midair. "Did you hear something?"

"No. I don't think so." Darcy shook her head. All she could hear was her pulse throbbing through her veins, strong with excitement.

"Well, then, what are you waiting for?" He smiled at Darcy.

"Of course." She nodded and moved in front of him. Her hand trembled as she reached forward into the dark, narrow space. Her fingers fell over a familiar object. "Feels like a book."

It was indeed a book. Her eyes swept over the cover, her heart practically skipping a beat as she read it.

Thomas raised an eyebrow at the item she'd pulled out. "It's a Bible. Why would he hide that? It's just like the one he had downstairs. The one I gave you to take to the hospital."

"No. This one looks less worn. Maybe like it's never been used."

Thomas lifted the book from her hands and shook it from the binding to see if anything had been tucked inside. A key and an envelope slipped out from between the pages and fell to the floor. Darcy swooped down and scooped them up. She turned the items over in her hands. Neither was marked and the envelope was sealed.

"Wait," Thomas whispered, putting a hand to her shoulder. "This time, I'm sure I heard something. Stay here."

Darcy nodded and watched as Thomas glided across the loft then slinked down the stairs.

Thomas came to a sudden halt at the bottom of the stairs. Someone was there. A man. Tall and slender. He was dressed all in black, including a stocking cap over his head, which prevented Thomas from being able to see his face.

"You're trespassing," Thomas said, stepping closer. The man was big. But Thomas was bigger. Much bigger. Of course, Thomas knew that the intruder could have a weapon, but there really wasn't much of a choice. He had to stand his ground and try to make this man leave. Then he had to get Darcy out of there. And call the police.

Without saying a word, the man pulled a gun from his jacket. Thomas could hear the hammer click to a ready position. He was going to fire.

Thomas stopped in his tracks, then dove over the sofa and hid behind it. The shot fired out. But it missed him.

Thomas scrambled to his hands and knees and peeked out from behind the furniture. The masked man aimed the gun at him again. Thomas shoved his hands up under the frame of the couch, grabbing on to the back of it with a hand at either end. It was even lighter than he'd thought. With a grunt he lifted the upholstered love seat and sent it sailing through the air toward the intruder.

The man lurched backward, trying to escape the giant projectile. The gun fired again.

This time Thomas felt something stinging through his flesh. He'd been hit on the top of his right leg. It wasn't going to kill him, but it stung fiercely. He howled and watched as the love seat crashed into the intruder, throwing the man off balance. The masked man stumbled backward and crashed into the wood-burning stove, knocking it over.

In an instant, the logs and embers that had been lit that morning to warm the team while they searched spread through the living space. The dry materials of Jesse's cottage caught fire almost instantaneously.

The intruder fled through the front door. Thomas hurried up the stairs. He had to get Darcy out of there. And fast. That old wood inside was going to burn like the sun.

Darcy had always heard that dry wood would practically combust given the proper conditions. It must have been true because that was exactly what seemed to be happening to Jesse's home. The cottage had suddenly become an incinerator.

"We've got to get out of here. Come on!" Thomas grabbed hold of her arm with such strength that she dropped the key and envelope.

Smoke already swirled through the loft. The flames would soon follow. Keeping his grip on her arm, Thomas pulled her to the edge of the stairs.

But then he stopped. The bottom of the steps was already knee-high in flames. There was no way out.

Darcy stared into the flames. Thomas hobbled around her. Why was he moving so stiffly? Then she saw his leg. A hole in his trousers. Fresh blood.

"Thomas, you've been shot!" Panic filled her words. This was all her fault. They should have left the cottage when everyone else had. Now how were they going to get out of there?

"I'm fine," he insisted. "Let's focus on getting out of here for now."

Get out? How could they? The only way left was out the window. "Please tell me Jesse has a ladder under the bed," she said.

Thomas hobbled away from the stairs toward the one and only window in the loft, pulling her along with him. "No. But I know how we can improvise one."

They reached the small window. Thomas yanked the curtains away from the wall and handed them to her. "Tie those together. End to end. Make the knots strong."

Darcy dropped to her knees and set to the task at hand. The smoke was growing thick. Thomas limped away again toward the bed. He grabbed the sheets and bedding and tossed them to her. He caught her looking at the window. "Don't open it yet. As soon as you do, flames will get sucked up here with us."

Thomas came back to her side and worked the other pieces of the cloth, tying ends together as quickly as he could.

Darcy coughed and tried to cover her mouth and nose with her starched apron.

Thomas tested each of the knots. He tightened a few of them and when he seemed satisfied he wrapped one end of the makeshift rope around the bottom leg of the highboy, then pinned a good portion of the material under the leg of the massive piece of furniture.

"It might not hold me all the way down, but it will definitely slow the fall and that's all I need."

He opened the window. Fresh oxygen was sucked into the house with amazing force. Darcy braced herself against the wall. More smoke rolled through the bedroom, following its new escape route to the outside. Underneath, the heat felt as if it would liquefy the cottage altogether.

Thomas threw the tied pieces out the window. They reached a little more than halfway down the side of the house. Not quite a real ladder, but better than nothing.

"Okay. So you go first," he said.

Darcy froze. "I—I—can't."

"It's fine. Just wrap the material around you and lower yourself down."

Darcy could feel her head shaking. She couldn't jump out of a second-story window. Not even with a blazing fire at her back. "Wait. Jesse's Bible."

She bent over and scooped their findings into her hands and clung to them.

He positioned Darcy at the side of the window. "Okay. Sit down and swing your legs over the ledge."

She sat and slung one leg over the window ledge and then the other. Thomas took the bedding and swirled it once around her left leg. He took the Bible, key and letter and tossed them outside. Then in one quick motion, Thomas grabbed her off the ledge of the window and started to lower her.

Darcy closed her eyes. Her heart was pounding. The quilt around her leg tightened slightly as he lowered her.

"Grip the quilts and slide," he coached her.

Darcy held her breath. She opened her eyes and looked up. Smoke was swirling around Thomas's head. She had to forget her fears and move quickly so he would have time to escape, too.

The makeshift rope held. She slid down it until she was only ten feet from the ground and then she let go and dropped the rest of the way to the ground.

Wasting no time, she turned around and called to him, "Okay, now, your turn."

Darcy was safe. Thomas let out a sigh. Part of him wished he'd just carried her down with him. She didn't weigh that much and then he'd be down there, too, instead of in this inferno with a bleeding leg and a head full of smoke.

The old cottage was burning at an incredible rate. He doubted they would be able to save any of it. Flames ravaged the dry wood like a hungry wolf.

He had to get out of there now, but getting his body through that tiny window was going to be much more of a challenge than it was for Darcy.

Thomas wrapped the quilt around his good leg. He checked the knot around the high boy. Then he put a hand on either side of the window frame and pushed himself through, feet first. His weight tested the makeshift rope. Thomas slid fast. Too fast. The quilt was slipping from inside. His fingers were losing their grip on the outside.

The thick material ripped through his hands then ended. His shoulder and hip slammed into the side of the house. He bounced out and away from the cottage. The ground was rising up to meet him. He tucked into a ball and tried to break his fall with a roll.

"Thomas? Are you okay?"

He felt his lungs fill with air again. He felt the feeling come back to his body. Pain. His leg was screaming with it. But he was alive, and so was she.

He opened his eyes to find Darcy perched over him on

her hands and knees. She was staring right into his face. "I'm going to be fine," he said. "How about you?"

"You saved me. Again." She grabbed his hand and tried to help pull him up.

Thomas lifted his torso off the ground and sat up beside her. They both looked down at his leg.

"It's going to be fine," he told her. "Can you go get my phone? It's in the buggy. We need to call the fire department."

"Of course," she said. But she didn't move away at first. Instead, she put her hands on his cheeks and leaned close to him. He could feel her soft breath on his face.

Thomas could see and feel the emotion in her huge eyes as they searched his. Without thinking, he cupped her cheek in his big hand and leaned his head into her, touching their foreheads together.

"Thomas," she whispered, like a warning. She dropped her gaze away and started to pull back.

His heart pounded. He tightened his hand on her and he pulled her to his lips. They were soft and warm and for an instant he forgot about his leg and the fire.

And then she was gone, running around to the front of the house, no doubt to get his phone from the buggy and call 911.

FIFTEEN

The fire department came quickly and doused the rampant flames, but not before the front porch fell in. Tomorrow they could comb through the ashes and see if anything was salvageable, but from the looks of it that was doubtful.

Thomas's leg has been treated. He moved easily now, but Darcy imagined there must still have been some pain.

She, too, had been to the EMS vehicle. Fortunately, the stitches in her forehead had stayed intact and she'd gained nothing worse than a few bruises. She sat now on the front bench of his buggy, where Thomas had wrapped her in heavy blankets. But she couldn't stop shivering. Mostly from the cold, she told herself. And perhaps a little from residual fear. But she also knew it was from Thomas, from his gentle touch. From his kiss. She could feel it still as he breathed against her. He'd tasted sweet, like apples. His beard had brushed against her chin. He had kissed her. And she didn't know what to make of it. If anything…

She watched Thomas while he talked to the firefighters, the police and the EMS team. He moved with self-assurance, seemingly unruffled by the chaos that surrounded them. A man of great strength, both physical and emotional. A man she hardly knew really, but who'd agreed to help her through this nightmare with no hope of getting anything in return but this headache of problems and a bullet through his leg. And he had kissed her.

A kiss she really needed to forget about. Thomas couldn't possibly be interested in her romantically. No way. He was so…Amish. And she was not. The kiss was just one of those things that happen in an intense moment. That was all. Nothing more.

What she really wanted to concentrate on was the Bible, envelope and key they had found in Jesse's highboy. She was too anxious to open the envelope to wait for Thomas to be able to join her. He probably wouldn't care.

Darcy picked it up. She slipped a finger through a gap between the flap and the top edge and ripped it across the top with her finger. There was a single sheet of paper inside. She opened it to find a typed letter with an old photo tucked inside. Another Polaroid—the exact picture Jesse had shared with her weeks ago. Her as a small child, with both of her parents. But this was clearly the original as opposed to the copy, on regular printer paper, that Jesse had provided. The photo had yellowed and faded with age. But there she was being held between the mother and father that she never knew. Darcy turned her attention to the letter and read.

It is not destroyed, but hidden where only the righteous and pure of heart may find it. These places hold the answers and the beauty and the destruction of the responsible.

After those cryptic words, there were two quotes that didn't make any sense to her.

Darcy shook her head as she read the letter through a second time, her heart sinking into her gut. Then she folded the paper back around the photograph and slipped them back into the envelope.

"How are you holding up?" Thomas appeared at the side of the buggy.

Darcy nearly jumped from her skin. She had not seen him walk over. "I'm fine."

"We can go home now." He climbed into the buggy beside her and pulled up the brake. His leg brushed against hers and the contact sent a shiver up her spine. She scooted over an inch to make more room for him.

With a couple of clicking sounds and a light tap of the long leather reins, his horse set off in a fast high-stepping trot.

"How's the leg?" she asked.

"It's nothing. I've had worse from falling off a horse." The warm sound of his voice resonated deep inside her.

"When we get home, Nana can you fix a hot bath. She also makes the best apple pie in the world."

"A bath sounds nice. But what would I change into?"

"Abigail may have something else for you to wear. And you can borrow something from Nana in the meantime. It might not fit but you can't stay in that."

Darcy pulled the blankets tighter around her torso and forced a smile. "It's funny how after being trapped in a fire, I now can't seem to get warm."

Thomas didn't respond. Immediately, Darcy wished she had worded that differently. He'd shared his coat with her the day before. He didn't have a coat on now, of course. It had burned in the fire as had her wool wrap. So it sounded like she'd meant for him to put his arms around her again. Ugh. Why did a kiss make things so awkward?

Darcy cleared her throat. Time to move on to another topic. "It's a real shame about the cottage. Did Jesse have insurance?"

"The Amish don't—"

"Have insurance… Of course you don't." Darcy pressed her lips together. "Then how does Jesse get medical care?"

"The community has funds put away for such things. To cover unexpected costs such as Jesse's hospital bills, or for when a house burns down or gets damaged in a storm."

"That's amazing. You really take care of each other."

"Isn't that what we should do? Help those that we love?"

"Well, yes, it's what people *should* do. But trust me, I don't think too many people actually do it." Then again what did she know? She hadn't exactly grown up in a normal loving home. In any case, she didn't want to talk about. "I opened the envelope."

"I thought you might."

Darcy shrugged. "I didn't understand any of it. It was very cryptic. Some quotes. A weird message at the top. And a picture inside. It was the original of the same picture he gave me a copy of when we first met—him and me with my mother when I was little."

"Where was that picture taken?"

"I don't know exactly," she said.

"Maybe it's important."

Darcy frowned. "Thomas, I know you're trying to help me and I appreciate it more than you know. More than I'm showing you, but… I should just go. We should just call Agent Danvers—"

"Agent Danvers? Don't you mean Agent Ross?"

"Come on, Thomas," she said. "You were nearly killed today. I'm just putting all of you at risk by staying here. I can't keep doing that."

"I don't think that man today was hunting you," Thomas said. "He was looking around the house. And he definitely didn't mean to set it on fire. That just happened in the scuffle—"

"In the scuffle of him shooting at you."

"Well, now that the house is practically destroyed, I don't think they will be back again. They don't know where you are. And they wouldn't even recognize you if they did."

"Do you think Jesse had some of the art stashed away there, in the cabin?"

"If he did, then it's gone now or at least damaged." Thomas shook his head. "But no. I don't think there was any artwork there. The FBI team would have found it. Plus, if Jesse did keep all that artwork, I don't think he would have kept it nearby."

"Kind of like how he had the photos in a box all the way out at the well?" she asked.

"Yes, but the pictures aren't worth anything. Paintings worth millions of dollars? Well, you would think he would have put those somewhere really secure."

"Like a vault."

"Right," he agreed. "Anyway, don't call Agent Danvers. At least not today."

"Okay, I'll see what McClendon and Agent Ross have to say. I just don't want to put anyone in danger. I mean, look at you." She glanced down to his wounded leg. "Does it hurt?"

"This isn't your fault, Darcy," he said. "None of this is. Just remember that."

His voice was full of emotion, but for what she wasn't sure. For her? For Jesse? For the destruction of the cottage? For the discovery that someone he loved was a thief?

He was right. Nothing about this situation was her fault. But that wasn't the only thing she was thinking about. She was thinking about Thomas. Was she starting to have feelings for him? Her heart was pounding. Darcy had to remind herself to breathe.

"Would you let me have a look at it? The letter, that is."

"Of course you can. You're the one who found it. And you're right. We should show it to Agent Ross."

"Good. I'm glad you agree because I already called him and told him about it."

For someone who'd been attacked and nearly burned to death, Darcy was amazingly resilient. He liked that about her. Actually, Thomas liked a lot of things about Darcy Simmons. He liked her small frame and her huge round eyes, especially now that he could see them in all their natural beauty, uncluttered by dark makeup. He liked her quick mind and her outspoken opinions.

What he didn't like was that she didn't like to talk about God. He didn't like that she didn't understand that some people were willing to help one another without expecting anything in return. He didn't like that she was going to leave. Which brought him to the real doozy that he didn't like—that he'd kissed her. Of course, that was his fault, not hers.

A rush of emotions flooded through him at the thought—emotions he would repress and ignore, as they had no possible hope of further development.

Anyway, the kiss had been just an expression of thankfulness that God had saved them from the fire. That He'd delivered them once again from a dangerous intruder. Right. Thomas swallowed hard. Although holding her close might have filled him with a feeling that was not exactly thankfulness. Not that Thomas wasn't thankful, of course—he was. But he knew what had really happened. He had gotten caught up in the moment. That's what had happened. And what a moment it was...

"You must be exhausted," he said, forcing his thoughts in a different direction.

"I would imagine no more than you are," she said. "Thomas, what if the letter and the pictures and the key all lead to nothing? What if Jesse never wakes up? What will we do?"

A sadness swept over Thomas at her words. He wanted to reach over and draw her close. But he couldn't. He wouldn't go there again. Anyway, thankfully they were home. Nana was standing on the front porch looking at them like they were a pair of teenagers that had stayed out too late.

"I have been waiting and waiting. I heard all those sirens," she began. "And I saw smoke. What were you all doing over there? I thought it was going to be just a small investigation. You know Jesse wouldn't like all these people rummaging through his belongings..."

There was a distinct pause as they got close enough for Nana to see the condition they were in and then Nana started again. "Oh, my! What has happened to the two of you? You're covered in soot and it smells like—"

"The cottage caught fire," Thomas announced.

"With the two of you in it, from the looks of it."

"Wait until you see his leg," Darcy said as she climbed out of the buggy.

"Thanks for that." Thomas eyed her as she jumped down. There was a twinkle of mischief in her stormy gray eyes. *Ja*, he liked that about her, too.

SIXTEEN

When Darcy walked into the kitchen she looked clean and refreshed, except for her slightly soiled frock. Thomas, on the other hand, had not moved far from the stool, where he had his leg propped up. He still smelled of smoke and sweat.

"Elijah and Agent Ross are on their way. I think they have more news," Thomas said. "Nana left out some coffee and sandwiches. I guess Nana's clothes don't fit you?"

Darcy pressed her lips together and shook her head. "Is she not joining us?"

"No, she thought she'd be in the way. Do you mind serving?"

Darcy poured both tea and coffee and filled a plate with the turkey sandwiches that Nana had made. Thomas liked watching her work. Plus, the smell of food was reminding him of how hungry he was.

Darcy was just putting things on the table when Agent Ross entered along with Elijah and Bishop Miller.

"Bishop Miller?" Darcy tried to hide the surprise in her voice, but Thomas could still hear it. "I—I don't think I have enough sandwiches."

"Not to worry, Miss Simmons." The bishop's voice was

calm and kind. "Elijah and I were able to reschedule our deliveries. How's the leg?"

"Kind of sore," Thomas admitted reluctantly. He hated being physically weakened. *You can't protect her, farmer boy.* Agent Danvers's words could not be truer. Thomas clenched his teeth. He should not be so proud of his strength. "Please sit down, everyone. And forgive me for not getting up."

"We understand you found something in Jesse's house," said Agent Ross. "But before we take a look at it, Bishop Miller wanted to tell you something."

"Jesse…" Bishop Miller paused. "Jesse told me a little more than what I shared with you the other day."

Thomas and Darcy both exchanged a glance then looked back to the bishop.

"Darcy, your father loved you. Leaving you with your mother's parents ripped him apart. But your grandparents wanted custody and he thought with what he'd done that he would never be able to win a custody battle in court. Plus, it was a question of safety. And I can assure you, he felt guilty about your mother's death. But he prayed for you every day. No earthly father could have loved you more. And he always knew where you were. One of the agreements he made with your grandparents was that he was allowed to know your identity and whereabouts as long as he promised not to contact you until after your twenty-fifth birthday."

Darcy looked ready to burst into tears. But she had to have been relieved to hear more about her past.

"I turned twenty-five two months ago," she said.

The bishop smiled. "I know. Jesse came to me and asked me what he should do. He wanted to contact you but he was afraid. Not of any of the danger that's been happening—I believe he never would have considered contacting you if he'd thought it would place you in danger. He was afraid you wouldn't love him. That you wouldn't forgive him."

The bishop paused for a moment, giving Darcy a chance to regain her composure, which she looked quite close to losing.

"Anyway," the bishop continued, "he decided it would be better to have tried and failed than not to have tried at all. And that's all. I heard that he had taken a turn for the worse and I just wanted to tell you how much you mean to him in case he doesn't get the chance to do it himself."

No one spoke for another minute, as Agent Ross set up his computer on the kitchen table.

"Should we take a look at what you found?" Agent Ross said.

"Wait a minute," Thomas said. "Of course we will look at the letter and key but I just got to thinking… Well, even if these new clues lead us to the paintings, then what? Darcy and Jesse are still in danger. What can we do about Wissenberg? What about the people that helped him find Jesse?"

"You're right. That just as important, which is why I've been on Wissenberg's whereabouts 24/7. But he is gone."

"How can he be gone? Wouldn't he still be on parole?" Elijah asked.

"Yes, but that doesn't always keep people who are well connected from disappearing."

"So how do you figure out who is doing his dirty work for him?" Darcy asked. "Like who told Wissenberg where Jesse was in the first place?"

"Right, well, we've worked on that, too, but like I told Elijah, it's touchy when an FBI investigation involves another government agency. Everyone is sort of territorial. What I have been able to get is a record of all of Wissenberg's visitors and phone calls while he was in prison."

Thomas nodded to show he was following. "Anyone of interest on that list?"

"My biggest hope is the three visits from someone who didn't sign in properly. My team is looking through footage of the prison video surveillance tapes. We hope to match a face up to a name and go from there. We also have leads on Wissenberg's two sons. They left the country after their father's trial. That makes it harder to find them. But there is a money trail. I think we may be able to get that nailed down soon. And there's also an unregistered phone number that he called almost every week. There is no locator on the phone, which means the calls are being filtered through some sort of computer program designed to keep people like us from locating phones."

"But it's not impossible to track down the phones," Elijah said.

"No. Not impossible," Ross acknowledged.

It was all so complicated, Thomas thought. But he was thankful for Elijah's friend. It sounded as though he was doing everything he could.

"What about other angles? Like other people who were involved in the smuggling? Or other people who worked at the Gregorian?" Thomas suggested.

"Exactly," Elijah said. "I thought of that yesterday morning and called Frank. That's why I told you we have news."

Agent Ross nodded. "We are tracking down a woman named Lenore Moon. She worked for Jesse and for Wissenberg and was part of the art-theft ring. She went to jail for fraud but only for six months. We think she's changed her name and her look. We are trying to get a location on her. There were rumors of a romantic interest between her and Wissenberg. It's likely that she knew about the paintings that Jesse held back and could be in on this."

"Why would she wait until now to look for Jesse if she knew he had the paintings all this time?" Darcy asked.

"Probably because she couldn't locate Jesse without Wissenberg's help. Or needed him to provide muscle, which he wouldn't do until he knew he would get his cut. Or she had nothing to do with it. It's just a lead. That's what all of these are…just leads."

"The coffee is getting cold," Darcy said, needing a break from the conversation.

She had been listening and asking questions, but her heart was so full of emotion that it was all she could do to keep from crying. Part of her wanted to run out of the room and escape all she was feeling. The other part of her wanted to run to the hospital and tell Jesse that she forgave him. No part of her could bear to look at Thomas. She knew if she did she would lose what little bit of control she had left. And though they had been nothing but kind to her, she did not want to cry in front of these men.

Darcy left the table to pour the tea and coffee. She returned and placed the sandwiches on the table and passed out some plates and napkins. She felt a little bit more in control when she sat back down again.

"Let us pray," the bishop said. "Our Heavenly Father, hear our thanks. Hear our praise. Know we are Your people. Give us ears to hear Your will and guide us along the path of the righteous that we may be found acceptable in Your sight."

Darcy whispered the words of Bishop Miller as he said them. She said amen as she thought about the bishop's words. *Was she one of God's people? How could that be? Was this feeling inside her what it meant to be called to God?*

"Thomas, where are the things we wanted to show

them?" Darcy did not look his way as she stood again and began to clear the empty plates.

"On the counter by the back door."

Darcy went to get the items and spread them out across the table.

Elijah picked up the key and turned it in his hands. "Looks like a bank key. Or a mailbox key. And the letter?"

"It's just a cryptic line about something hidden and then a couple of random Bible verses," Darcy said. She read the first one aloud.

"'Next they made the courtyard. The south side was a hundred cubits long and had curtains of finely twisted linen.' There's no reference."

"That's from Exodus," Bishop Miller told her. "It's from the building of the tabernacle under the direction of Moses. Everything was very exact. Every inch of the instructions. Fascinating."

"What's the other verse?"

"It's just as fascinating," said Thomas. "Read it."

Darcy cleared her throat. "'He gave two carts and four oxen to the Gershonites, as their work required.'"

"And that would be from Numbers," the bishop said. "Still about Moses. But I believe this is dealing with offerings."

Agent Ross was typing into his computer. "I got the references," he said. "Exodus chapter thirty-eight, verse nine and Numbers chapter seven, verse seven. I'll have my team look into code possibilities."

He read the rest of the letter. "Most likely the top part is a message and the bottom tells us how to decode it."

"Well, if everything you need for the message is in the letter," Darcy said, "why also leave the Bible?"

"Right," Elijah said. "He wrote the verses out and specifically left off the references."

"And the key? How do we figure out where that fits in?" Thomas struggled to get up off the stool. Darcy flinched watching him move so stiffly. "I don't know about any code or secret writing. In fact, that all sounds a little too fancy for Uncle Jesse. What if it just is what it is?"

"Which would be?" asked Agent Ross.

"A bunch of numbers and instructions. Directions. An address."

"Telling us where to go to use this key," Darcy said. *And to how to end this nightmare.*

SEVENTEEN

"We will look at every possibility," said Agent Ross, packing up his notes and computer. "The FBI has the best cryptographers in the world."

Darcy appreciated Agent Ross's help, but she knew the FBI's top cryptographers would not be focusing all of their attention on a twenty-year-old art smuggling case. She was surprised he'd been able to help as much as he had. Surely he had other cases requiring his attention, and yet he had come up with several leads for them, and had come willingly to help whenever Elijah called. She just hoped one of the leads would pan out soon. Soon enough that she would not have to go into WITSEC. She couldn't even bear the thought of it. If only she could just go home. But after the break-in, home didn't feel particularly safe anymore. In fact, the only place she'd been in the past few days where she'd felt truly safe had been Thomas's arms.

Thomas walked the guests to the door. Darcy hung back in the kitchen. She was glad not to have to leave with Elijah and go back to the Millers' just yet.

But poor Thomas. She knew he was in pain. She also knew he had a lot of work to do—his regular chores on top of the preparations for the singing—and it would be extremely painful, with no one to help him other than his eightysomething-year-old grandmother.

"*Ach!* That was a long meeting and I need to be in my kitchen. So much to do for the singing tonight." Nana Ruth came busting into the kitchen. "And you, my dear, will need another change of clothes. You can't wear that old smoky thing tonight. I'll have Thomas phone Abigail. Hopefully she has another dress still hanging around."

Darcy looked down at herself. She had washed the grime from her hands and face before the meeting, but Nana was right. She smelled like smoke and fear, and her dress was streaked with dirt. And since Nana was about as wide as she was tall, sharing with her hadn't worked out. Darcy made a mental note to be careful from now on of how much Amish food she stuffed away while she stayed there. Hopefully, it wouldn't be for much longer.

"So, what can I do to help?" she asked.

"You can get out there to that stable and help my grandson." The old woman turned to her, her little spectacles sliding down her nose. She put her hands on her hips. "Don't wait for him to ask you for help. He never will. But he needs it."

"Of course," Darcy said. She hurried out of the kitchen and across the courtyard. The temperature had dropped dramatically. And somehow the inside of the barn seemed almost colder than the outside. She walked up and down the aisles. It was a large stable. She found Thomas hobbling forward with a wheelbarrow. "Tell me what I can do to help?"

"What? You? Come to help me with the horses?"

"Yes. Me. Why not? I'm already dirty."

He smiled. "Okay then, come on. I'll show you how to muck out a stall."

"I don't think there's too much to it," she said, grabbing the wheelbarrow away from him.

"Hey, I was using that to help me walk," he teased.

"You shouldn't be walking at all," she countered. But she couldn't stop him from following her from one stall to the next. She mucked. He filled the water buckets and placed blankets on some of the horses.

"What did you think about the meeting?" she asked him.

Thomas twisted his face in thought. "Lots of angles. Complicated. But I know Agent Ross is doing what he can. And the fire department and police will be back out at the cottage tomorrow. You never know, they may uncover something about that intruder that gives us another clue."

"I don't know. Whoever it is has been pretty careful so far. No prints at my house or Jesse's previously…though he might have been distracted enough today to drop something without meaning to. I can't believe you threw a sofa at him." She tried to picture the couch flying through the air.

"Well, it seemed only fair. He had a gun and I didn't." Thomas laughed and leaned against the wall. "I think I must have had a lot of adrenaline going. Anyway, it was a small sofa."

"Do you think we will ever figure out what that letter means?"

"If God wills it." He looked her dead in the eye. "Then yes, I think we will figure it out."

God… Is that who had led them to the message and the box with the pictures? Well, she hoped if He was there and listening that He would bring an end to this sooner than later.

Thomas watched Darcy dodge hungry horse heads over the stall doors. Getting around the stable with a shot-up leg was slow going and it hurt. He probably should have gone to the doctor, but there was no way he would leave Darcy and Nana alone at the house, unprotected. And now it was good to move around. He was certain Abigail would take a look at it when she arrived with another dress for Darcy to wear.

"This is the feed room. It stays closed up or critters will wander in. Now, we have several types of grains—some for horses in work, some for horses in foal and some for…" He looked back at her. "Well, you get the idea. So first we fill the buckets and then you distribute."

"Sounds easy enough."

Thomas handed the grain-filled buckets to Darcy and she put them in the wheelbarrow and rolled it down the first aisle. "We'll start here."

He handed a bucket to Darcy and opened the first stall for her to enter. She held the bucket loosely, between her thumb and forefinger. Thomas repressed his desire to smile.

"Watch out, now. This is Princess. She doesn't have very good manners."

Princess turned around and whacked the bottom of the bucket with her head. Darcy squealed. The bucket of grain went flying through the air and Darcy landed right on her backside.

Thomas pressed his lips together to muffle his laughter.

"You knew she was going to do that, didn't you?" She stood and brushed off her skirt.

"I was trying to tell you she has terrible manners. She was very poorly named," he said. "I'm sorry about that. But perhaps you'd do better to keep your eye on the horse and not on the ground."

"Point taken. But they didn't do that when we were mucking."

"You didn't have food in your hands then."

Darcy stood up and brushed her skirts off. Princess nibbled up the spilled grain around her feet. "She's beautiful, isn't she?"

"My most valuable mare," he said. "Would you like to ride her?"

"Me? Ride?"

"Yes, you. Ride." He crossed his arms over his chest. "One of my favorite things to do is ride bareback in the snow."

"Snow? What snow?"

"Oh, it's going to snow for sure."

"So you're a weatherman and a horse whisperer," she teased.

"I'm just a simple God-fearing man, Miss Simmons." He smiled and handed her another bucket. "Next up, Storm."

"Storm? If she lives up to her name, then maybe you should feed her."

They made their way through the barn. Thomas loved the flow of their rhythm. They didn't speak much, but still anticipated the movements of one another. It was like their hundredth time feeding the horses together, not their first. He couldn't help but think about the kiss, too. That had been foolhardy of him. Still, regret was not what he felt over it. It was more a feeling of grief that it could never happen again.

"I come bearing gifts." Elijah's voice sounded through the stable, loud and, to Thomas, a bit unwelcome as he knew his time alone with Darcy was now at an end.

"Back here," Darcy shouted.

Elijah came jogging around the corner. "A dress for you," he said to Darcy. "And pair of crutches for you," he said to Thomas.

"Any word on Jesse?" she asked.

"Abigail says he's steady," Elijah answered. "She will be here later to see this patient. As for you—" he turned to Darcy "—Nana said she will draw you a bath, but only if you hurry because then she needs you to help carry the food out to the barn."

"Thank you." Darcy hurried away.

Thomas should have thanked her but the words somehow stuck in his throat. He watched the back of Darcy floating away from him until she turned and disappeared around the corner of the stall. He didn't like watching her leave.

Remembering Elijah standing there, Thomas shook away his thoughts. He put a crutch under each arm and took all the weight off his bad leg. "Hey, these are great."

Elijah nodded readily.

Thomas swung his way to the stable office and lit a lantern. Elijah followed. "Let's go grab those benches."

This time, Thomas followed Eli out to the large trailer that housed all the church benches and tables. Every other week they traveled to a different home for Sunday church. And occasionally they were used for weddings and funerals and other events like the singing.

Tiny flakes of snow floated through the air.

"I knew it was going to start soon," Thomas said. "How much are we getting?"

"Maybe a foot." Elijah got into the trailer and slid out the benches.

Thomas put down his crutches and helped to set the benches on the ground. "You'll have to get one of the boys to help you carry them inside."

"No problem. I'm sure some kids will start showing up here in no time."

"I'm glad for the singing. It's good to get our minds off Jesse and these break-ins."

"And the fire," Elijah mumbled. After unloading the trailer, he hopped down. "Do you think Darcy can keep her cover with a whole barn full of Amish?"

Thomas nodded, trying to keep his facial expression neutral. "*Ja*. She's pretty, uh…pretty good, *ja*?"

Elijah slapped his friend on the back. "I saw the way you looked at her."

"The way I looked at her?" Thomas tried to play dumb. "You mean a worried look."

"I wouldn't call what I saw a look of worry," Eli teased.

"What would you call it then?" Thomas sighed and picked his crutches back up.

"I'd call it a look of admiration. Affection. Thomas, I'd call it chemistry." Elijah smiled, but his eyes were focused, making it clear that Thomas should listen closely.

"Chemistry?" Thomas repeated casually. "Elijah, I think you've been smelling too much shellac at the furniture store."

Eli's smile went flat. He was not joking and he wanted Thomas to know it. "I suppose I'd only call it chemistry, if I didn't know better. But I do. The Thomas I know is much too smart to fall for an *Englischer*, even if she is all dressed up in a nice plain frock."

If his friend could see through him, who else could? He would have to be more guarded. More careful with his eyes and his attentions.

Thomas met Elijah's eye. "Advice taken."

"Now, go get cleaned up before that *Englischer* uses up all the hot water."

A little while later, Thomas tried rinsing the smoke and an entire day's worth of grime off his aching muscles. It wasn't easy to keep the bullet wound dry.

Darcy had helped him today, but he'd have to get his cousin's son to come lend a hand in the stables for the next few weeks until he healed. After washing up, he dressed in a clean white shirt and his best pair of trousers. He ran his fingers through his dark curls and then down his beard. Darcy was right. It had never grown in too well. It was strange that she had asked him about it. When his marriage had not worked out, he had wanted to shave it off, but his father had said that was not the way.

Thomas had never kissed a woman since Mary. Not until today. He supposed over the past ten years he had never met one he wanted to kiss. And now that he had, she was an *Englischer*. Elijah was right to remind him. There was no future with Darcy. Thomas knew that and he needed to act accordingly.

Darcy couldn't remember when a hot bath had felt so good. She only wished she could have lingered in it a little longer. It had been fun working the stable with Thomas. But she could tell she was going to be sore tomorrow from all that shoveling. And sore from falling out of a two-story window.

After toweling off, she dressed in another of Abigail's frocks. She combed out her hair, parted it and pulled it back. She fit the white prayer *kapp* on her crown, surprised at how quickly she'd grown accustomed to dressing herself in these clothes. It wasn't easy. There were no buttons. No zippers.

Next, Darcy lifted the lovely silver locket and turned it over. There was a small inscription on the back:

Forever yours, October 4

She wondered what the date could be. Their wedding? The day they met? Ten…four. The number date made Darcy think about all the numbers in the verses that Jesse had written in the note she'd found. She wanted to get her hands on that Bible. She disagreed with Agent Ross about the letter being a code in and of itself. She was certain that the letter and the Bible had to work together. She just needed some time to look through the Bible. Find the verses. Study the pages. Maybe, just maybe, something would pop out at her.

Darcy fastened the locket around her neck and slid it under the collar of the dress, then hurried down to help Nana Ruth with the evening's festivities.

EIGHTEEN

It was after six o'clock when the kids had started to show up in groups and pairs. Darcy and the Miller family had placed tables and benches and plates and mugs and napkins out. Nana had made obscene amounts of food. The whole time, Darcy had wrung her hands and worried.

It was one thing to disguise herself as Amish when she was with people who knew she wasn't like the Millers and Abigail. It was another to keep up the act in front of a whole community of Amish folk. There were over thirty Amish teenagers plus friends and family gathered in Thomas's indoor paddock for what everyone called the "singing."

The boys were lined up on one side of the table and the girls on the other. The girls outnumbered the boys almost two to one. But no one seemed discouraged. Most of the adolescents had arrived in small open carriages and carts. Others had walked through the snow. With no musical instruments for accompaniment, the adolescents began to sing songs of praise and worship, sometimes in harmony, sometimes in unison. Sometimes in English, sometimes in Pennsylvania Dutch. Their glorious voices lifted to the roof and beyond. Darcy couldn't remember when she'd heard anything so wonderful in her entire life. All her worry and fears melted away with their voices.

"Gelobt Sei Gott im hochsten Throne... Hallelujah, hallelujah, hallelujah...

"Praise God on the highest Throne... Hallelujah, hallelujah, hallelujah."

"We haven't had a singing here for a while," Thomas told her as he sat down beside her.

"It's wonderful," Darcy said. "At first, I couldn't believe these kids came here through the snow to sing worship songs. But now that I see how much fun they're having..."

"I'm glad you're enjoying it. You know, there are usually at least ten more kids attending. So I do think the snow may have stopped a few from coming. But at least our place is more centrally located than the home of the family who was originally going to hold the singing tonight. Nana got wind a few weeks ago of someone wanting to relocate, so here we are."

"And it's the finest barn in Lancaster County," said a tall boy who had just entered. He shook hands with Thomas. A frail dark-headed girl stood shyly behind him. "Thanks for having it here. You saved my parents." He looked to Darcy and tipped his hat.

"I'll take that." Darcy reached for the fresh bread in his arms.

"Thank you, ma'am," the boy said with great enthusiasm. "I'm Amos Beiler. And this is my girl, Lucy King."

"Nice to meet you," Darcy said.

"Now, go join the fun," Thomas urged them. As they walked away, he leaned over to Darcy and whispered, "They will get married come next November."

"They're engaged?"

"No. They won't announce it formally until the end of the summer. But they've been steady for years."

"For years? They look so young."

"Lots of couples marry at eighteen or nineteen. It's not so young when you're already working and making a living."

"So I guess I'm pretty much an old maid according to your standards?" she asked.

"The oldest," he teased.

Darcy gave him a sideways glance and punched him in the arm.

"But don't worry. None of the boys will ask you to go for a buggy ride after the singing. They all think you're with me," he said. His gaze was on her, obviously waiting for a reaction. She'd give him one. But it wouldn't be the silly girlish blush that he might be expecting. Yes, he had kissed her. Yes, she was attracted to him. But she and Thomas were like milk and soda—not ever meant to be together.

"Well, maybe you should set them straight." She stood with Amos's bread in her hands and a flat expression on her face. "I'll go put this on the table with the others." She scurried away from him to the food table.

Thomas used his crutches and swung over beside her, closer than he needed to. His scent wafted over her, a mixture of manly musk and homemade soap. Whether he was the soda or the milk, there was no denying his appeal. His fingers brushed her upper arms, sending a chill through her entire body and something else. Something she hadn't felt in a very long time—in fact, maybe it was something she'd never felt.

"Meet me outside," he whispered through the thin layer of her prayer *kapp*. "I want to share something with you."

Her heart beat wildly. What could it be? He must have had news about the intruders or about Jesse. Whatever it was it sounded good. Darcy put the bread on the dessert table with the other treats. She and Nana had made several gallons of hot chocolate for the kids, too. Nana stood guard by the table, refilling mugs and loading plates with cakes and cookies.

Darcy grabbed a wool wrap that Abigail had brought over for her and threw it around her shoulders. As she walked through the aisles of the stable, she wondered if Thomas had heard from Agent Ross. Maybe he had figured out the verses in the letter. She passed through the front door and out into the courtyard.

Thomas stood a few feet outside next to one rather large gray horse. The horse was bridled but wore no saddle. His light-colored coat shimmered like stars in the night. Thomas looked as handsome as a movie star. He wore a smile that was brighter than the blanket of snow covering the ground.

"I thought I'd better get you out here in the snow before you decided to go on a buggy ride with one of those fine fellows at the singing. How about a ride?"

"Me?" Darcy shook her head slightly. What was happening? "I—I was expecting information about the case, not... But what about your leg?" She looked down at the ground. Her heart was racing. Her hands trembled.

"No information. Sorry. Just me and a horse. But I'm not going to ride. Just you."

"Just me? Oh, I don't think so. I don't ride," she informed him. "No way."

"Well, not really all by yourself. I will lead him. You just get to sit and look pretty."

"Thomas, I don't know... Shouldn't we stay and oversee the singing? You are the host."

"*Ach*, no." He waved his hand through the air. "Nana's inside. Anyway, we are riding patrol."

"Patrol?"

"Ja." His voice was mocking, so she knew his words weren't the least bit serious. "Sometimes the couples want some alone time. They wander off into the woods for a kiss or two."

"Sounds like you know from experience."

"Maybe." He winked, smiled again and waved her to him.

"What if I fall?"

"Are you going to fall?"

"No."

"Gut. And just in case, I brought you a helmet." He placed the rider's helmet on her head and fastened it around her chin.

"Well, there's one more problem." She put her hands on her hips. "I'm wearing a dress, in case you hadn't noticed."

"You think Amish girls don't ride horses?" He paused for a moment. "Well, they don't too often actually. But it's not unheard of."

"Okay, fine. I give in."

"Here, let me give you a leg up."

The next thing she knew Thomas had slung her over the back of the horse. She balanced herself and took hold of the reins. Thomas put another halter over the horse's head and connected a lead rope to it.

"How do you feel?"

"A very long way from the ground." She glanced over her horse's shoulder toward the snow-covered ground.

Thomas grinned. "He's a gentle giant of a plow horse. I'd put my own baby on him."

Darcy hadn't ridden horses since she'd been to summer camp as a girl and she'd never ridden bareback. Nor in the snow under the stars. She had forgotten how much she'd loved it.

* * *

"You have ridden a horse before." Thomas couldn't take his eyes off Darcy as she sat astride the big gray. She was tense and clung onto the horse's reins but she kept her head up and her legs still. He only wished he could have ridden, too.

She laughed. "I haven't been on a horse since I was thirteen at summer camp. My grandparents sent me every summer. It didn't take me long to realize that they were just getting rid of me for the summer."

"That must have been hard. Not knowing your parents. Having grandparents that weren't close."

"Oh, don't feel sorry for me. My grandparents spoiled me. Anything I wanted, I got."

Except love, he thought.

"I'm glad you brought me out here."

"Me, too." Thomas stopped and stared up at her. He was falling for Darcy Simmons, harder and deeper each moment. Did she feel at all like he did?

Not that it mattered. She would go home soon and he had to remind himself of that. This wasn't her life. He wasn't going be anything to Darcy. And she wasn't going to be anything to him. Anyway, who would be stupid enough to fall in love with someone who was destined to leave him? He'd already done that once. He certainly wasn't going to do it again.

Darcy looked back down at him. "You okay? Your leg must be killing you. We've walked a long way and you're only using one crutch."

"No. I'm good. Abigail took a look at my leg and said the EMS guy did a really good job cleaning it up. It really was just a graze."

"You don't feel pain, do you?"

"Oh, I do." He saw a movement in the distance. He turned his head to follow it.

"Are you sure you're okay?" she asked again.

"Yes, I just thought I saw something in the woods." He shook his head. "It was probably just a deer."

And yet, Thomas was pretty sure what he'd seen was on two legs. It might be nothing. Or it might be someone dangerous, come to harm Darcy again.

He turned the horse around and led them back toward the barn as fast as his leg would allow. The stable glowed like a beacon as a light snow fell. The singing was a faint hum in the distance, floating over the snow-covered fields. It was a terrible thought to consider that danger might still be lurking at their doorstep. And why *his* doorstep? He searched the woods again. All seemed still. He was just tired and imagining things. After all, who would risk coming around with all these people here?

Darcy didn't seem to be listening. She was staring up at the night sky. Her face glowed in the soft moonlight as a few lucky snowflakes kissed her soft skin.

"Did you ride a lot with her—your wife?"

His wife, Mary? Mary was the furthest thing from his mind. "What made you think of that?"

She shrugged. "I don't know... It's just sort of romantic, I guess. You know, the barn singing. The ride in the snow."

"No. Mary didn't ride." His jaw tightened. "She didn't really like much about life in the country."

She looked down at him and smiled apologetically. "I shouldn't have asked. But..." She hesitated, and he figured she was torn between good manners and curiosity. Finally curiosity won. "It's just that you seem so content. Aren't you sad? Aren't you angry that you lost your wife? Aren't you lonely?" The words came out in a rush, and as soon as they were out, she looked uncertain. He figured she was worried she'd said too much, and he hastened to reassure her.

"I don't mind talking about Mary. I am very sad that she died so young from cancer. But the saddest part is that she spent so much of her life unhappy. Not because of me, but because she didn't want this life. Her family pressured her to take vows and marry. She wanted to leave here. And eventually, she did. Not long after we married. You see, she got sick after she left me—not long after she finally had the life she wanted."

"Wow." Her eyes were wide. "How you can be so okay with that? Didn't that hurt? I don't know anyone who could talk so calmly about someone who treated you like she did. How could she have done that to you?"

"It's called forgiveness," he said. "It's a way to show love. Sometimes when you love something, you have to let it go. It's the only way to have peace in this life, Darcy. Love and forgiveness."

She pressed her lips together and nodded. "I've never met anyone like you. Like all of you—your friends and family. You're all so…accepting. So comfortable with who you are."

"How about you?" he asked. "Any lost loves? Someone special in your life now?"

"Ha. No. Never. I go on a lot of first dates."

"So, you're content being single, it seems. I'm not so unique after all."

"No. I'm not. I'm not content. Or at least I haven't been." She looked off into the distance.

Thomas stopped walking. He turned around and looked up at her. Tears filled her eyes. A few had spilled over her lids and down her cheeks. It pained him to see her hurting. He wished he had not asked her.

"I am so sorry. I did not mean to upset you," he said.

"No, it's just that when Bishop Miller told me about my father, that he asked for my forgiveness. It dawned on me how different my life would have been if I had had my father in my life. If I had lived here with him instead of my grandparents. I had…"

"Had love?" Had *Gott*, he thought, but did not add. God was working in Darcy just fine without his interference. Maybe there was no future for him with Darcy. But there was one for her with God and for that he was so glad she had come here.

She nodded and turned to him, her face streaming with tears. "Can you imagine? What if he had brought me here with him like he'd wanted to? Then I'd have been…"

"You'd have been loved," he said. *And Amish*, he thought to himself, *and not off-limits to me*. "But you are loved, Darcy. You have friends. You have an important job."

"I have a good life. But Thomas, I've never been happy." She pointed to her heart. "And I never really knew it until I came here, because I didn't know there was more. Seeing life through the eyes of you and your people, it makes my world seem so small and unimportant and empty." She chuckled at herself. "I sound crazy, don't I?"

Thomas reached up his arm and closed his fingers over her hands that clutched the reins. "Crazy? No. You do not sound crazy at all. You sound like you have found *Gott*. And in *Gott* you are finding peace."

She laughed again and wiped away the tears. "Maybe you're right…"

He let go of her hand but he didn't want to. "Accept what you have found, Darcy. Never let it go. It won't matter where you are or who you're with."

They rested in silence for a moment. Darcy wiped her eyes and looked away, then she stiffened, causing even the docile plow horse to stir.

"What is it?" he asked.

"You were right, Thomas." Her voice was as cold as the air around them. "Someone *is* in the woods."

NINETEEN

Darcy sat rigid on the back of the giant draft horse. Her tension no longer had anything to do with riding bareback or finding God. She had seen someone in the woods.

"It could be some of the kids from the singing," Thomas suggested. But she could tell by his stern expression and the way he'd quickened his step that he knew it was an intruder. *The intruder.*

But how? She understood an intruder at Jesse's, or at her town house, but here? At Thomas's? Why would they come here?

"Oh, no," she cried. "Thomas, where did you put the Bible and the other things we found at Jesse's?"

"Agent Ross took them," he said. "Why?"

"Because why else would someone be here?"

The intruder at Jesse's cottage had fled the house and the flames, but he might not have completely fled the scene.

"What if the man who shot at you stayed near the house during the fire and watched us leave? What if he saw us throw those things out of the window to save them? What if he knows we have that key? And what if he already knows what to do with that key"

"Slow down, Darcy."

"No. Thomas, the person I see is running. And he most definitely does not look Amish. Do you see him?"

Thomas followed her gaze. She could see his expression of concern amplify as his eyes found the dark figure.

"*Ja.* I see him. Here, Darcy." He lifted up an arm. "Slide down. I'm going to go see who it is."

"After he shot at you?" Darcy slid off the big horse. "You can hardly walk. Plus, what if he has a gun again?"

Thomas wasn't even listening. She might as well have been talking to the horse. She knew Thomas well enough to know that he wasn't going to let anything happen to all those people at the singing. They were under his roof and they were his responsibility. And so was she. He was going to keep them all safe and if that meant his leg hurt or he got shot at again, he most likely didn't care. Why was it that the thing you admired most in others could also be the thing that drove you crazy about them?

She wanted to grab his arm and hold him back, but even with Thomas being wounded, she was no match for his strength. She watched as he slid the halter off the horse and handed it to her. He took the reins from her hands and with teeth clinched he swung himself up on the back of the horse. His face betrayed the pain that had to be rippling through him. He'd probably reopen the wound.

"Go back inside, Darcy. I'll be right back."

He clamped his legs around the huge gray and he galloped toward the forest's edge.

At the same moment, shrieks sounded from inside the barn and then there was a sound a bit like rolling thunder. Darcy had never heard that noise before, but instinctively she knew it was horses. A lot of horses, all moving together in a herd.

A large door where the gathering was taking place slid open and about ten of the horses came barreling out. They bucked and ran and whinnied and snorted until they'd all exited and then, like horses do, one of them stopped and so did the rest. The boys from the singing were already running after them with lead ropes.

Darcy glanced back at Thomas, who looked back at the commotion. Her heart raced wildly. Maybe he would come back now? The intruder was probably long gone anyway. But Thomas kept moving away from the stable.

Thomas heard and saw the commotion back at the stable, but he didn't stop. There were plenty of boys at the gathering who could tend to his horses. Darcy would be safe if she went back toward the others. And to keep them all protected, he knew he had to keep going.

He had easily closed more than half the distance between the runner and himself. But they were getting close to the highway now. If there was a car waiting, Thomas feared he might not make it in time to stop the intruder.

"Stop! You're trespassing!"

The runner looked back. Thomas saw his face, reflecting in the bright snow-lit night. It was not anyone he knew and yet his face seemed familiar.

Thomas saw the man's car parked at the edge of the woods. There was a creek several yards from the road and only one good place to cross. The man had not parked near enough to it to make his escape. Thomas clamped on to his mount and clicked his tongue against his cheek, urging the steady horse to increase speed and jump the creek. He'd forgotten the pain in his leg.

Thomas pulled up on the other side and cut the runner off before he reached the car. The man slipped and slid in the snow right under the horse's belly, but was not able to escape as Thomas jumped down and grabbed the man by the collar of his black coat.

The man stood and turned to him with his head dropped. It was a man he'd never met before, but he looked so much like an image he'd seen on Agent Ross's computer screen that Thomas knew that it had to be Wissenberg's son.

"Going somewhere?" he asked the man.

"This is not what it looks like. I promise," the man said. "I was trying to stop her. She's crazy."

"Who's crazy?" Thomas asked.

"My sister."

Darcy broke into high gear and arrived at top speed at the open barn, throwing her helmet aside. On her way, she passed a few able adolescents who had rushed forward to catch the loose horses. Most of the kids had backed up along the sides of the indoor paddock. One or two others had not been fortunate enough to get out of the way before the horses had run through. Darcy checked these kids first. A couple of scrapes and bruises, but thankfully no one had been seriously injured, mostly just frightened. Some of the grown-ups, including the Millers, had stayed on and were helping attend to the frightened kids.

Darcy scanned the room for Thomas's grandmother. Nana Ruth stood back near the entrance to the main stable. She looked unharmed.

"Are you okay?" Darcy asked. "What happened?"

"I don't know," said Nana Ruth. "All of a sudden the door to the aisle was thrown open and ten or twelve horses came running through. It was madness."

"Did you see anyone suspicious inside the stable? Did any of the kids wander away from the group?"

"No," answered Nana Ruth. "I kept track of the children. Everyone was here and accounted for except for you and Thomas. Thankfully the kids had stopped singing and lined up close to the table for more food and hot chocolate. Otherwise there would have been many more injuries. Where is Thomas?" Nana's brows knitted together in a deep frown.

"He saw someone running into the woods. He went after them on the horse."

Nana whispered something under her breath that Darcy couldn't quite understand, but she knew it wasn't anything good.

"I'm going to go check the rest of the stable." Darcy turned away.

Nana grabbed her by the shoulder. "Take one of the boys with you. I don't think you should go in there alone."

Darcy scanned the large room for Amos. Nana was right. She shouldn't go into the stable alone. She was just so used to doing everything herself. Having people around that watched her back was a completely new experience for her.

She just hoped that the dangerous people who were after her wouldn't hurt any of these good people. If they did, she would never forgive herself.

Darcy spotted Amos helping some of the girls to the benches. She hastened toward him and asked for his help. Within a minute, they had passed through the great door and into the main aisle of the stable.

The horses that were still inside their stalls twitched their ears and showed the white in their eyes. They paced to and fro at the doors of their stalls. Their anxious calls of distress reverberated through the hollow barn.

A large whip had been thrown in the center of the aisle. Amos stopped and picked it up.

"I suppose this is how the intruder herded those horses through a closed door. It is a good thing the door lifts as well as slides, or it would have come down completely," said Amos. "That would have hurt even more people."

A *clippity-clop* sounded behind them. Darcy jumped, thinking someone had let out another horse. But when she turned to look back, she relaxed. Some of the teens were bringing in the horses that had escaped. The animals were restless and fearful, but the Amish teens were experienced and patient as they soothed them back into their proper homes.

"Everything looks fine," said Amos. "I think someone played a prank on us."

Darcy didn't believe that for a second. This was all because of the artwork and her and Jesse... Clearly, someone thought he still had them and was willing to do anything to get their hands on them.

Darcy shook her thoughts away. "There's two more rooms at the other end. I want to check those, too."

Amos followed her down the long aisle to the stable office. She was surprised to find the feed room door wide open and the lids off of all the food bins. The floor, too, had a thin layer of grains spread all over the floor.

"I'll clean this up," Amos said.

"Thank you, Amos. Do you think there's anything stolen from in here?"

"Sometimes people steal tack but I never heard of stealing horse feed," Amos said. "But I guess people are always surprising us."

Darcy nodded. "Do people play pranks like this often?"

"No, ma'am. But you know how *Englischer* kids can be."

Darcy forced a smile. She hadn't lied about being Amish, but she felt like she was lying by wearing their clothing. "I'm going to check the office. Be right back."

Darcy walked the remaining steps to Thomas's office. That was where he had told her he kept his tack and anything else of value. The office door was also open and clearly it had been forced as the bolt had ripped through the frame of the door and splintered the wood. Darcy peered inside just as someone dressed in all black came flying through the office doorway. He plowed her down and made his escape through the far doors.

TWENTY

"Just give her the artwork," the man said to Thomas. "Or she's liable to dig up your whole community and she won't care who's in her way. And she especially won't care about Finlay's daughter. She knows the daughter has the key. And she knows you know where the daughter is."

Thomas squared up his shoulders. His mind was reeling. His leg was bleeding. His brain was trying to make sense of what this man was telling him. "You're Wissenberg's son?"

"I'm nobody," the man said. "A friend."

"You're on our side? Then why were you running away if you're here to warn us? Why should I trust you?"

"You should trust no one." With a sudden motion, the man pulled his arms together and took advantage of Thomas's momentary surprise to break free. He pushed Thomas backward. Thomas caught his heel on a root and fell back to the snowy ground.

Before Thomas could recover, the man raised his knee high to his chest and with a look of pure evil on his face rammed his boot down into Thomas's wound. Agony ripped through Thomas's whole body, crippling him for a good few seconds. By the time he stood again, the man was in his car on the other side of the road. The wheels spun and he revved his engine until the car sped away across the new fallen snow.

Thomas tried to read the license plate. But he could only make out that it was Canadian and started with the number six. Thomas looked back to the stable. He didn't know how much to believe of what the man had told him. He clearly had gotten Thomas to let his guard down so that he could get away. He hardly seemed trustworthy. On the other hand, Thomas didn't want to completely dismiss the possibility of there being a second intruder still threatening the safety of the folks at the stable. If the man was telling even a bit of the truth, it meant that Darcy's life was endangered over the key they had found. The key that wasn't even in the stables. But, of course, the intruders didn't know that.

Thomas looked for his horse. The animal had jogged several yards away from the scuffle, but now stood like a steed of war waiting for his rider to march back to battle. Thomas found a felled tree near the creek and used it to help him remount. It hurt to move his leg in any direction, but riding on a horse with four good legs would be a lot faster than a man walking on one with a gash in the side of it.

He clamped his teeth down and fought the pain. He should have listened to Darcy and gone back to the stable. He only hoped he wasn't too late and that his mistake wouldn't be the cause of injury to anyone else. Especially Darcy.

Darcy squealed as she went down flat on her back into the middle of the stable aisle. Amos raced out of the nearby feed room and saw the fleeing man in black.

"Are you hurt, miss?" he asked.

"I'm fine," she said.

"I'm going to get that kid," Amos said running after the man in black.

"Wait! No," Darcy grunted, trying to refill her lungs with air. But Amos leaped over her and chased after the intruder.

Darcy pulled herself up off the ground and followed behind. Amos was stopped at the large front doors to the barn. "He disappeared. I chased him out of the stable, but when I got here...nothing."

Darcy searched the ground. There should be footprints in the snow, right? But the ground revealed nothing but a confusion of boot prints going in every direction. There was nothing to glean from the snow.

"It's okay," Darcy said. "It probably wasn't wise to run after him anyway. But thank you for helping. You're a brave kid."

"You think we were in actual danger?" He turned to her with a look of surprise.

"The stampede was a massive diversion so that they could search Thomas's office," she said. "They didn't seem to care too much about hurting any of us. Yes, I would call that dangerous."

"But what could Thomas have in his office worth all of that?" Amos asked.

A key to a pile of stolen art worth ten million dollars, Darcy thought to herself.

"Nothing," she answered. "There is nothing in the world that could be worth that."

And it was the whole reason she knew what she had to do next...

Darcy and Nana sat on one side of the kitchen table, each having a cup of herbal tea as they hoped to calm their nerves. Elijah and Chief McClendon sat on the opposite side of the table sipping coffee. Thomas was back on his stool with his wounded leg propped up high. Abigail had cleaned the wound again and redressed it. This time she told him that he was confined to the house and should sit or lie down for at least the next twenty-four hours. She had given him a shot of antibiotics in the hip, which had hurt almost as bad as the cleansing. She'd tried to talk him in to a mild painkiller, but he had refused. He needed to keep his head clear.

He did, however, ask Amos to take care of his horses and the stable for the rest of the week.

McClendon took notes in his little electronic pad. He wrote down descriptions of the intruders and he took multiple accounts of the activities from various community members before all of the guests had scattered.

Most of them had left believing the whole affair had been the work of some rotten and thoughtless teens. But a few of the visitors had started connecting Jesse's beating, the fire and now the stampede with the possibility that something much more sinister was taking place. Thomas didn't know what the bishop had told those few inquisitive folks, but at this point everyone had gone home and Thomas knew that meant the others were away and safe.

"I should have canceled the singing after the fire," he said. "I didn't think the trouble would follow us here."

"What's done is done," said Nana as she pushed away from the table. "And *Gott* doesn't want us to go around living our lives in fear and regret. No one was seriously hurt. No broken bones. No trips to the hospital. That's all that matters. Now, I'm going to bed. I don't think I'll sleep a wink but I'm going to try. If you will all excuse me."

"Yes, ma'am," everyone said.

"Did you catch the model and color of the car?" Mc-Clendon asked.

"No, I didn't catch the make," Thomas said. "But it was a dark color. Maybe gray or blue. It had four doors. Looked new. Canadian plates—Ontario, I think. I only caught the first number. It was a six."

Thomas shifted his weight on the stool. McClendon typed in a few more notes. Everyone looked exhausted and weighed down.

"Can anyone think of anything else?" McClendon asked.

They all shook their heads. They'd been over everything. Every detail of his encounter in the woods and the escape of the intruder in his office.

"Then I will take Eli and Miss Simmons back to the Millers'. Let's call it a night," McClendon said. He looked at Elijah. "We can phone Agent Ross from the car and get him up to speed. I'm going to post a car here, Thomas. From the sounds of your conversation in the woods, these people will be back looking for the key since they didn't get it tonight."

Thomas had the strangest sinking feeling as the three of them said goodbye. He dismissed it as emotions born out of exhaustion and confusion and the pain ramming through his leg. He wanted to say a private good-night to Darcy. He wanted to finish the conversation they'd had under the stars. He wanted to go back to that moment when he'd held her hand on the reins and she'd shared her heart with him.

But he knew he couldn't. She wouldn't even look back at him as she left the house.

Thomas knew it was better that way. But that didn't matter. Knowing something is right doesn't always make it feel better. Sometimes knowing what is right was just sad. Thomas made his way slowly up the stairs and into his bedroom. He lay across the quilted covers, too lost in his thoughts to draw them back. He turned out his lantern and closed his eyes. But, like Nana, he knew he wouldn't be able to sleep.

Darcy sat quietly in the back of the chief's car, knowing exactly what she needed to do. She listened to Elijah speak to Agent Ross over the phone. She knew they were all doing everything they could to help. But it wasn't enough to stop the danger.

Her presence and this mess of her father's were putting others in harm's way. And Darcy was determined to put a stop to it.

Whether or not the attackers on her trail knew she was there dressed in Amish clothing was unclear. But it wasn't something she was going to bank others' lives on. If she left Willow Trace and made it obvious that she was back at her town house, then the focus of the hunt would resume there and she could know that these people were safe—that Thomas was safe. As they pulled into the Millers' drive, she realized she needed to make her move now.

"I'm going to leave," Darcy announced to Elijah and McClendon. "Please call a taxi for me."

"What?" McClendon said. "I don't think that's going to help anything. Where are you going to go?"

"Home."

"Alone? That's not safe."

"Am I free to go?" she asked.

"Well, of course you are," the chief said. "I just don't think it's advisable. You are safer here."

"Maybe I am. Maybe I'm not. But for sure everyone else is safer without me here."

Neither of them argued with that reasoning.

"I just need to go inside and change back into my own clothing. If you could call a taxi for me, I'd really appreciate it."

"Sure," McClendon said. "I'll call one now."

Darcy headed into the Millers' house to get her things. Elijah raced after her.

"Why are you doing this?" he asked.

She didn't answer. He knew why she was doing it. "Does Agent Ross have the letter and the key and the Bible that we found yesterday? And the box of photos?"

"Yes, he took all of it," Elijah said. "Well, except for the box the photos were in. Why?"

"I just want to keep with me something that belonged to my father," she said. "Could I have it?"

He nodded.

Darcy changed into her own things. She spread the frock she'd worn over the quilt-covered bed. She ran her fingers over the plain cotton fabric. She placed the black apron over the front and the prayer *kapp* at the collar. Heavy emotions welled inside her.

Her own clothing felt tight and restrictive against her limbs. She said a quick goodbye to Hannah and to Bishop and Mrs. Miller. Elijah waited for her outside. McClendon had already left and the taxi had arrived. In his hands, Elijah was holding the beautiful wooden box that Jesse had made. He handed it to her. As she grasped it in her hands, she felt peace. She was doing the right thing by leaving.

She smiled at Elijah. "Take care of Thomas," she said.

"You're not coming back, are you?" he asked.

Darcy put her hand on his shoulder. Emotions swelled in her, rising so high that all her thoughts and words swam in them. She couldn't answer him except with her eyes. She climbed in the taxi and closed the door. She had one more goodbye to make. This one at the Lancaster General Hospital.

Then Darcy knew she would never be back to Willow Trace.

TWENTY-ONE

Darcy sat next to Jesse in the ICU. She held his limp, cold hand in hers. The poor old man clung on to his life by a thread. She spoke softly to him. She doubted he could hear, but there were things to be said all the same.

"I don't know why you kept those paintings, Jesse. *Dad*. But I do know you must have had a reason. Thomas believes in you and, well, so do I.

"It's been a crazy few days finding out about the truth. About you and Mom. I understand why you and Grandma and Granddad made the decisions that you did after Mom was killed. And there's nothing to forgive. So you don't ever have to ask. You should know that I always loved you. Even when Grandma wanted me to be angry with you the way she was. I didn't know enough to understand what had happened, but now that I do, I know that you loved Mom. You did the right thing by testifying. And you did the right thing by writing to me."

Her eyes filled with tears. She wiped them away with her free hand. "I can't stay long. But I had to say goodbye. And don't worry. I'm going to make sure that Wissenberg knows I've been to my house so that none of your friends will be in danger anymore. I will make Wissenberg think that I have the key and everything else he wants, even if that's not true, and then—then I'm going to disappear. They will know that I'm lost to them forever and with me, the hopes of ever finding the paintings. But I love you. I'm so, so glad you wrote to me. Wake up, Jesse. And know I love you."

Darcy wasn't sure but she thought she felt Jesse's hand tighten just ever so slightly around her fingers. "Thank you, Jesse. I'll be thinking of you."

Darcy stood. She bent over and kissed her father on the forehead. She had so much to thank him for. She would never forget her time here in Willow Trace. She would never forget the people and their kindness and their love for God. She would never forget her friendship with Thomas and how his quiet strength and faith had helped lead her to a budding search for her own peace. She knew she didn't fully understand God's love yet, but she had felt the power of its force in brief waves around her and she wanted more. Her heart was open and ready.

Wiping away one last straggling tear, Darcy headed for the door. She wasn't two steps outside Jesse's room when she came toe-to-toe with a familiar face.

"Agent Danvers." Darcy stopped fast as tall agent was blocking the way. "What are you doing here?"

"I figured you'd be back to see him sooner or later," the woman said. She ran a hand over her blond spikes.

Darcy wasn't sure if she wanted to trust the US Marshals office. After all, they had completely failed Jesse. But Danvers was there and…well, she knew she didn't want to be alone in her town house. "I guess you read my mind."

"So you've finally come to your senses and decided to relocate?"

Darcy nodded.

"That is a wise, wise decision." A wide smile stretched

across the agent's face, which seemed more filled with triumph than compassion.

Darcy looked back toward Jesse's room. Already, some of her newfound peace felt as if it were eroding. She didn't want to give him up, but she knew that she had to. She was doing the right thing for everyone. But if that were so, why did she feel so unsure?

Sleep would not come. Thomas sat up in his bed. His leg was throbbing and his mind raced with thoughts of Jesse and Darcy and the fire and everything else. He might as well get up and focus on something constructive.

He relit the lantern and grabbed his Bible. He looked up the two verses that Jesse had put in the letter. Exodus 38:9— *Next they made the courtyard. The south side was a hundred cubits long and had curtains of finely twisted linen.*

Thomas reached again to his side table. He picked up his journal and pencil. He turned to a clean page and started scribbling. *Three, eight, nine.* The reference numbers. But there was a number in the verse, as well.

He skipped a line, then wrote *one hundred*. But wait, he thought. It's not a just a hundred. It's a hundred cubits. In the footnote of the Bible, it stated that would be about one hundred fifty yards. Maybe the number he wanted was 150? But 389 what? And 150 what?

Then he wrote the verse from Numbers. Chapter seven. Verse seven. Seventy-seven. *He gave two carts and four oxen to the Gershonites, as their work required.* Two carts and four oxen. That could be six if he added the numbers or it could be twenty-four if he just wrote them side by side. But again twenty-four what?

Thomas scratched his head. *Not what*, he thought. *The question isn't what. The question is where.* Where the artwork was. Like he'd thought before. It's not a code. The verses provided an address. Some combination of these numbers provided a zip code or a street number or maybe even the postbox or bank number where the paintings were.

Then Thomas remembered what Darcy had said about the Bible being a part of the message. If the verses and the numbers were all that was needed then why had Jesse hidden the Bible, too? That only made sense. Thomas flipped back from one verse to the other. This wasn't Jesse's Bible, but it was the same edition. If something was important about the Bible, surely the intended message would be on the same pages as the two verses.

Thomas read the pages. He studied them. Something was there staring right at him, but what? Page numbers? Maybe. He scribbled those down, as well.

Thomas wrote the numbers several different ways. It was a lot of numbers. Too many for a zip code. Too many for a street address. But what other way could one locate something using numbers?

Coordinates. If he took the verse reference numbers and added the triple-digit page number to each of the verse reference numbers then... Thomas wondered if it was about what you needed to give a very precise longitude and latitude. He wasn't sure, but thought maybe a little time on a computer would help. Of course, he didn't have one. But Abigail did. He hated to wake her after all the help she'd been earlier at the singing, but this was important.

Thomas pushed himself off the bed and hobbled down the stairs and out to the stable, where he usually kept his phone. He was going to get this figured out.

Tonight.

* * *

Agent Danvers had been quiet as they walked out of the hospital. Darcy paid the cab driver who she had asked to wait. She took her things out of the backseat, then followed the agent to her truck and climbed in. The drive to her town house seemed interminably long. The snow had stopped and the main roads were completely clear, but still it seemed like they were moving at a snail's pace. Darcy had asked Agent Danvers what would happen when she relocated. What were all the people she knew going to be told? What would her design team think? Her boss? The US Marshal had not been too forthcoming with her responses. Something about it all being explained to her later.

Darcy knew she was doing the right thing. But she already missed Willow Trace. She missed all the friendly faces. She missed Thomas. She hadn't even been able to say goodbye.

Finally, they arrived at her town house. Darcy unlocked her car and took out the Bible that had belonged to Jesse— not the one he'd hidden away, but the worn one he'd obviously read regularly. In all the commotion of the last trip to her place, she had forgotten to take it to read to Jesse in the hospital. But she was glad she'd forgotten now, because she had it to read herself. To learn more about God and also as a keepsake to remind her of Jesse and Thomas.

The first thing Darcy did when she got inside was turn on her phone. She wanted Wissenberg and whoever his little minions were to know that she had left Willow Trace. She got on her computer and answered several emails, too.

As she now rummaged through her town house, gathering the few things she wanted to take with her to her new life, Agent Danvers kept rushing her. In fact, the woman paced her living area, and was biting her nails and constantly talking on her phone in whispers. Darcy couldn't figure out what she was so nervous about. Darcy was the one who was giving up her life. Not Agent Danvers. Danvers was just doing her job. Shouldn't she be used to this sort of thing?

When Darcy emerged from her bedroom, she found Agent Danvers hovered over a huge mess on her coffee table. "What are you…?"

Darcy paused about halfway across the room. She could see what was spread out over the table. It was Jesse's box. The woman had completely disassembled it.

"What did you do that for?" Rage rushed through Darcy's veins.

"I knew there had to be more than one key," Danvers said. An evil smile spread over her lips. She reached down over the table and lifted up a small key.

Darcy stumbled back a step. Why would Agent Danvers be looking for a key?

"It's a place in Washington, DC," Abigail told Thomas over the phone.

His heart pounded. "This must be where the paintings are," he said.

"I don't know, Thomas," Abigail said. "It's some sort of restaurant and bar."

Thomas thought for a second. "Well, I may be off a little. I thought my Bible was the same edition as the one we found in Jesse's highboy. But it's possible that it's not—meaning the page numbers could be slightly different. We need to call Agent Ross."

"I don't have his number," Abigail said. "I'll have to call Elijah and I doubt he's going to answer his phone at this hour. In fact, I doubt he even has it in the house with him."

"You answered."

"My husband's an ER doctor. We always answer the phone," she said.

"Then we will just have to drive over there," Thomas said.

"*We?* Thomas, it's the middle of the night. This can wait till morning."

"I don't know, Abby," Thomas felt his pulse racing. He felt a sense of urgency that he couldn't explain. "I got this feeling that we need to take care of this tonight."

"Go back to bed, Thomas," she said. "I'm getting another call."

Thomas decided he would call Elijah himself, even though he knew Abigail was right. There was no way his friend had his phone on and inside the house. Eli's father, the bishop, tolerated phones for business and emergencies, but he wanted them out of the home whenever possible, which when you got right down to it was most of the time.

Elijah's line went to voice mail and Thomas left a detailed message explaining his theory about the location. He wanted to hitch up his buggy and ride over to the Millers'. He especially wanted to share what he'd discovered with Darcy. But Abigail was right. He knew that a buggy ride would be slow and painful with his leg hurting so much, and the Millers would hardly be happy to see him at this time of night. It could wait a few hours. It would have to.

Thomas pushed himself up and started to go back to the house, when he heard his own phone ringing. Maybe Elijah had kept his phone nearby and had heard the message? It wouldn't have surprised him with all the excitement that they'd had the past few days if Elijah wanted it close in case of another emergency.

But when he looked down at the phone, it wasn't Elijah's number calling. It was Abigail. He answered.

"Change your mind?"

"No, I didn't change my mind," Abigail said. "That was Blake on the other line. He called to tell me that Jesse woke up."

TWENTY-TWO

Abigail did come to pick up Thomas and the two of them hurried to the Millers'. But not so much to tell Elijah about the coordinates, as to tell Darcy that her father had woken up. Jesse was going to live. What a blessing!

The coordinates didn't even matter anymore. Now that Jesse was awake and alive, he could tell them everything. This was all going to be over. Darcy would be safe.

"I'm glad I have a key," Abigail said, as she exited the car and skipped up to the front porch. Thomas stayed in the car to rest his leg.

Abigail let herself in and disappeared into the dark house. About three minutes later she reemerged not with Darcy, but with a dress and apron in her hands.

"She's gone," Abigail said. "The bed's made and my dress was laying right across it."

Thomas felt the worst sinking sensation travel from his head to his gut. He opened the car door and started to climb out. "Where's Elijah?"

"I'll go get him," Abigail said. "Hannah is going to kill me for waking them up."

"And I'm going to kill Elijah for letting Darcy escape," he said. Of course, he didn't mean it. Elijah couldn't keep her there if she'd wanted to leave. He was just so upset. Hurt. Why would she leave? How could she leave? Without even saying goodbye...

"You're not really a US Marshal, are you?" Darcy felt nauseous, as if she could faint.

"Just now figuring that out?" Danvers snapped.

"Then who are you?"

"What's it to you?" Danvers said. "You'd be dead already if I didn't need you to open the mailbox."

"Mailbox? You know where to use the key?"

"You don't?"

"No."

"You left us all the clues," Danvers said. "The ones your dear old dad left for you."

"But you don't have them. An agent at the FBI has them," Darcy said. "And you don't have the key, either. That key only works on the box. The one you just broke into a thousand pieces."

"I have friends in the FBI," she said smugly. "Friends who work in Cryptography. I couldn't get my hands on the key. It was held in a different department. But I got the address and I bought myself some time before that Agent Ross who you got involved will find out about it. And as far as your key goes...well, you're right. One of the keys works on the box. But you and your handsome farmer friend didn't look hard enough. Your father was too paranoid to have just one key in one hiding place. There was another one. And I found it."

Darcy had to admit the key did look just like the one they found in the highboy. "How did you know to look in the box?"

"You and your friend were pretty loud at the cottage."

"That was you?" Darcy said. "You shot Thomas?"

"Yes, but I missed the fatal shot I was aiming for and I really don't like it when I miss."

Darcy looked around her home. Could she run? Could she make it to her car? Maybe she could cut through the back and escape down the alley. If she could get her phone, she could call 911. But she'd left it back in her bedroom.

"I need to get something," Darcy said, turning toward the bedroom.

Danvers quickly pulled a pistol from her phony US Marshals coat. "I don't think so. I think you're going to be sticking right next to me until the post office facility opens up at eight o'clock tomorrow morning. Now, let's go. We got a little driving to do."

"The coordinates point to a mailing facility in northern Virginia," said Elijah after hanging up the phone with Agent Ross.

"Not a restaurant," Thomas said.

"No, you didn't have the right Bible. The one Jesse left has slightly different page numbers, so that shifted the exact location slightly. Anyway, Ross is going to drive down there right now. He said it would take about three hours."

"What about Darcy?" Thomas asked.

"No one can get a hold of her. She's not answering her phone."

"Anybody call the US Marshals?"

"You think she went with Danvers?"

"I hope not. But maybe she thought it was the only way to stay safe?" Thomas rubbed his scraggly beard with his hand. "What about the taxi driver? You said she left in a taxi. Can he tell us where he took her?"

"Worth a try."

Elijah lifted his phone and within a couple of minutes,

he was speaking with the driver. Thomas could hear his friend using every means of persuasion that he could to get the driver to talk to him. Finally, he clicked off. "She went to the hospital. Stayed about fifteen minutes then came out, paid the fare and left with a woman with short, spiky blond hair."

Thomas took off his hat and twisted it in his hands. What were they going to do?

"I'll call Agent Ross. I don't think Agent Danvers would take a call from us, but she wouldn't be able to ignore another federal agent."

"It's worth a try," Thomas said, trying to slow his pounding heart.

"And relax," Eli said. "I'm sure it's not too late. It's only been a few hours. We'll get her back with her dad in no time."

Elijah turned away with his phone again. Thomas hoped his friend was right. He hoped they weren't too late to stop Darcy from making the biggest mistake of her life. He wished there was something else he could do... besides just rely on Elijah's connections. But he was thankful they had them.

Elijah's eyes met Thomas and his friend dropped the phone to his side. "There's no Agent Danvers working in the US Marshals."

Agent Danvers held the gun at Darcy's chest and Darcy froze. She didn't even dare breathe. She couldn't believe she'd been so stupid to think that it was normal that Agent Danvers was hovering around her father's hospital bed waiting for her to show up. She couldn't believe that none of them had suspected the so-called agent earlier back at the hospital, when she acted so nervous and over important. No wonder she seemed so callous and flippant about relocation. She wasn't even an agent. She was a criminal and she'd sat in on a meeting with the Lancaster chief of police without anyone suspecting.

Suddenly, there was a loud knock at the door.

"Our escorts are here," Danvers announced. The fake agent pressed Darcy toward the front door. Darcy opened it to find two huge men standing there.

"Miss Simmons," Danvers said, "meet my two brothers. They've been kind enough to volunteer to escort us to Virginia. I wouldn't have even worried about it if it weren't for that meddlesome farmer and his friend. But I have a feeling they may come looking for my truck and me, which is why we're going to take your car. At least, part of the way."

Darcy studied the two men. She remembered Thomas's description of the guy in the woods that he'd caught. Thomas had said he looked like a young version of Wissenberg. Well, so did these two guys. In fact they looked so much alike they could be twins, and they strongly resembled the man she suspected to be their father. Now that she was looking for it, she realized Danvers looked like him, too. Especially if she didn't have the fake blond hair, but the smoother darker hair of her brothers.

"Well, they're my half brothers," she added. "Different mother."

Wissenberg's family. How nice of them to all work together, she thought.

Danvers took a set of keys from one of the men. "Go get her ID and car keys."

One of the men disappeared into her home while Danvers pushed Darcy through the front door, gun at her back, and led her to the passenger side of her red car.

"You didn't think I'd let you drive, did you?"

Danvers handcuffed Darcy to the passenger door. Apparently, she hadn't bothered to lock it that night she'd left with Thomas and Elijah. She truly had been in a state of shock. She wished she had left the Bible in the backseat. The one that belonged to Jesse. It would have helped to calm her nerves. But still she remembered the words of Bishop Miller. She was a child of God. He would take care of her. And she believed it.

God, I know I don't know You too well. But I'm trusting You'll help get me out if this. If You can.

And Thomas always said that anything was possible, *if it's God's will.*

Danvers walked around to the driver side. One of her half brothers came running out with her clutch bag. He handed it to Danvers, who clawed out her keys and threw the bag at Darcy's feet.

Her clutch. Darcy's heartbeat quickened. She didn't expect that God could answer her prayer so fast. But He had. He had given her hope.

Yes, the clutch had her ID in it. It had her car keys in it. It also had her phone in it. Unless they'd been smart enough to take it out. She hoped they hadn't been. She hoped the guy was as stupid as he looked. And she hoped that the phone was still tucked away in its little zippered compartment.

"We will be a few cars back," the man said. And off they all went. Danvers drove frantically through her little town and then even faster once she got to the highway. Darcy felt bile and adrenaline roiling through her. She was nauseous. What did they need her for?

"So where are we going?" Darcy asked.

"South," she said.

"I can see that. Anyway, why do you need me?"

"Only you or Jesse can get to the postal box. Even with the key, it's in a secured area. Anyone allowed access has to have ID."

"What are you going to with me afterward?"

"Take you for a little swim," Danvers said.

"So is your name Wissenberg, too?"

"Anyone tell you you ask too many questions?"

Darcy took that as her cue to fall silent, though her thoughts kept racing. She just wanted to get her hands on her phone and get help. But would she have a chance before this madwoman ended her life?

Thomas thought he had felt every sort of emotion there was, but what he experienced now he had no words for. It was more than panic. More than rage. It was some sort of combustible power inside him that he knew folding his hat over in his hands would never soothe away.

"We have to do something," Thomas said.

"Agent Ross is sending a car for us," Elijah said. "He's going to have us meet him at the heliport. It's the only way we can catch them. They have a huge head start on us."

"They're going to let us go with them?" Thomas knew that had to be completely due to Elijah's friendship with Agent Ross.

Elijah nodded. "Agent Ross said any man smart enough to figure out that address without any cryptography training is welcome on his team anytime. Anyway, he needs you."

Thomas gave his friend a doubtful look. "We're pretty sure Danvers has the address. But we don't think she has the key. One of us will have to have a trade-off of Darcy for the key."

"And what if they do have a key? What if they don't need us?"

"Pray that they do," Elijah said.

TWENTY-THREE

Agent Danvers pulled off the interstate and followed a winding single-lane road for about three miles. Darcy was growing more and more worried. This was not how she'd imagined the drive to the secure box. It was much too rural. She'd held out some hope that if they were in a busy area, she might be able to give her captors the slip, or at least call out for help. But out here, no one would hear her.

They passed a gas station and a cluster of old motels. One had a diner in the front of it named Mickey's. Danvers pulled into the parking lot.

"Are we stopping to eat?" Darcy asked.

"No."

"Good. Because it doesn't look very good." Darcy's sarcasm was just a weak outlet for her fear.

"Shut up." Danvers pulled Darcy's red compact car in next to a brand-new luxury sedan—a Mercedes that was sleek, black and loaded. "I'm going to move you to this other car. And I'm going to make a pit stop."

Danvers reached over and released her handcuff. "Don't run. My brothers are right beside us."

She wasn't kidding. The giant twins were pulling in just on the other side of the Mercedes. Darcy reached for her clutch. She got out and walked to the other car. One of the brothers casually got out of his car and waved to her like they were old friends.

"Susan, it's so crazy running in to you here."

Susan? What was he talking about?

"Let me get the door for you," he said. "Oh, look. I think you dropped something."

Click!

Darcy realized he had just come over to lock her in the car, and that the faux casual chitchat was his way of making their interaction look natural in case anyone in the diner was watching. This time she was handcuffed to the seat. Not her hands but her ankle. He shut the door in her face. "So good seeing you."

Danvers was busy grabbing a bag from her brothers' backseat. Then she disappeared into the diner.

Stay calm, Darcy told herself. She reached into the clutch and felt around the side pocket. Her heart leaped with joy. The phone was there. She pulled it out, careful not to look down at what she was doing. She didn't want to alert the twins to her discovery and what she hoped would be her rescue.

Thomas could feel his phone buzzing in the seat beside him. He hated that he would have to let go of the armrest to see who was calling. He knew holding on to the armrest gave him a false sense of security, but it was nice to have the assurance all the same.

He was buckled tightly into a seat on a small helicopter. Agent Ross was across from him, as was Elijah. They were on a quick path to Alexandria, Virginia, and to a secure and private lockbox facility located at the exact coordinates that Jesse had cleverly hidden within the confines of a letter and a Bible.

The helicopter ride—the first he'd ever taken—was

noisy and unsettling to his stomach. But he couldn't say he didn't find it intriguing. He imagined being this high up was a little like seeing the world through God's eyes. Some of it was so beautiful. But some of it not. Most of what they could see now was nothing but highways everywhere, a concrete jungle he'd once heard someone call it.

Thomas picked up his phone and tried to ignore the ground and sky that flashed by him as he read the display. It was Darcy. He couldn't believe it.

"She texted," Thomas yelled to Agent Ross. "She wrote, 'It's Danvers. With her now. Please help.'"

He held the phone over for Ross to look at. Ross took the phone in his hands. "Hold on while I get a lock on her location."

Ross spoke over some sort of radio system that only he could hear. "My team is locating her. They've also got an ID on this Danvers. I asked the hospital to send over the security tapes from the other day when you all met in the conference room. Since Darcy is in such immediate danger, I want to find out as much as we can about what we are dealing with. The facial recognition came up fast. The woman's name is Kelsey Moon. She's the illegitimate daughter of Wissenberg and Lenore Moon. She changed her name to Danvers so that no one would associate her with her mother or father since they'd both been in prison. When she turned eighteen, she joined the army. She served a term in Afghanistan as a ranger, but was dishonorably discharged for stealing documents from an officer's computer. She's a trained killer. And we think she's teamed up with her twin half brothers on this venture to steal back this stolen art. The license plate you saw last night could very well belong to Remy Wissenberg, who we found lives in Ontario under the name of Rossen. It seems all three of the children changed their name to slow or divert anyone from discovering connections they had to their father and—in Danvers's case—her mother, too. But all the while they stayed in touch. The other twin moved to Europe. We were able to trace the computer-generated calls to his location in Lublin, Poland, which is the birthplace of Wissenberg's father."

"Nice family," Elijah said.

Ross held up a hand as more information was coming through. Then he yelled something to the pilot and the chopper changed directions sharply.

"Okay. We're heading in. Five minutes to destination. We're going to get her."

Thomas grabbed at his stomach, as the aircraft pitched and swooped. But the rest of him had hope. They were going to find Darcy. And get her away from this killer.

Darcy spent one second too long getting her phone back into the zippered part of her purse. Danvers caught her red-handed.

"Idiot!" Danvers yelled, only she looked nothing like the Agent Danvers from before. She'd changed out of the monochromatic pantsuit and replaced it with a stylish pair of black dress slacks and a sexy blue sweater, which clung to her thin body like a wetsuit. The spiky blond hair was gone, revealing her true, long, flaxen locks.

She grabbed the phone from Darcy and threw it into the street. Then she got into the driver's seat. She reached into her bag and pulled out her gun. With the gun in one hand and the other hand steering wheel, they pulled out of Mickey's parking lot and back onto the one-lane highway.

"Thomas, this is going to be okay," Elijah said. "Darcy is going to be fine."

Agent Ross smiled as he tucked a weapon away in a

holster under his arm. "He's right. We've got her location and we are one minute to touch down at that diner. We may not even have to use the key as bait. This will be a total ambush if Darcy has been able to conceal her phone from her."

Thomas hoped—no, he prayed—that Ross was right. He could let Darcy go back to her *Englisch* life if that's what made her happy, but he couldn't lose her like this. That he just couldn't live with.

The chopper passed over a patch of forest, then a river and another patch of forest. They began to descend through an opening in the trees. Thomas saw a group of buildings and a highway running through the middle.

"There's her car!" Thomas saw the small red compact in the lot on the other side of the street.

"He's gonna set down here," Ross shouted. "More space."

The pilot was busy maneuvering the helicopter. He leveled it out, then they went down almost like they were connected to a rope and bucket in a well. Thomas kept his eyes on the car. Was it empty?

"I don't see anyone," he said. "Maybe they went inside."

"What's that on the ground next to the sports car?"

"It's her phone," Ross answered. "That's what the GPS tells us."

The chopper landed. People from the diner began to come out and see what all the noise was about. Ross hopped out of the chopper and ran toward Darcy's car. He was shaking his head. He walked toward the crowd of people at the door and flashed his badge. A second later he was sprinting back to the chopper. He jumped back in and waved his hand in a circle. They lifted up into the air again. Ross took his seat.

"They are already gone. We need to get to that post office." Ross clenched his teeth, his face tight. So much for the ambush.

* * *

"Put this on." Danvers handed Darcy a long black winter coat, a pair of sunglasses and a white knit ski cap. Darcy did as she said and about two minutes later they pulled into the mailing facility located on Moses Road. The strange message at the beginning of Jesse's letter didn't seem so cryptic anymore. It seemed Moses had been guarding the paintings all along, just like the letter had said.

Danvers had her pistol on Darcy's back as they walked inside. The facility was one of the bigger nationwide shipping companies that boxed things for individuals or companies. Only this one was private and offered a second layer of security for their box rentals.

She had done plenty of business with places like this working for Winnefords. It was sometimes faster than the regular postal service. In the back of the store was the counter where their staff packed, weighed and labeled shipments. In the front of the store were hundreds of PO boxes that people rented, instead of receiving mail at their homes or offices. And to the side was a private locked chamber, where you could secure valuables without going to a bank. Darcy imagined it was frequented by some pretty shady customers.

Danvers directed Darcy to the checkout desk. "Hand him your ID and tell him you want to open box twenty-four. Here's the key."

Twenty-four. Two and four. That had been a part of the verses, too. Jesse had left every needed clue in his letter. She just hoped that Thomas got her text and that Agent Ross knew where to come. She prayed. Because if they didn't get there soon, her life was going to be over.

Danvers pressed the key into her open hand. "And don't try anything. Even if you get away from me, my brothers are watching."

Darcy did as Danvers said. She placed her key on the counter and showed the man her ID. She couldn't believe it when the man typed some information into her computer, then smiled.

"Hello, Miss Simmons. It's been a long time since you've been to your box. But you are still paid up through next year."

"I'd like to have access today, please."

"Of course." The attendant came out from the cashier stand and escorted them to the private chamber of rental boxes. He pressed a code in the keypad and the electronic door slid open.

"You have five minutes to exit," the attendant said and then turned back to the line at the cashier stand.

Darcy looked around the giant mailing facility. Danvers wasn't going to try anything here. There were too many people and too many cameras. Still, the phony agent kept the concealed weapon at her back and edged her into the chamber, where there were rows and rows and walls and walls of boxes.

Darcy knew each one of the walls would have a box 24. They'd have to hurry if they wanted to try them all in five minutes.

She moved forward toward the first row of boxes, but Danvers steered her roughly in another direction. "It's this set of boxes."

It was numbered 150. "I thought the other verse had the number *one hundred* in it?"

Danvers pushed her forward. "So you *did* understand the message."

That realization seemed to make Danvers nervous. She had been pushy before but now she seemed in a downright panic. "Give me the key back," she growled, ripping it from Darcy's hands.

She pulled Darcy along with her to box 24 of aisle 150. She inserted the key and slid out a large cylinder. It was made of a unique type of wood and it was locked. Now what?

Apparently, Danvers didn't care about this step. She looked triumphant as she shoved the huge piece at Darcy.

"Carry it out to the car," Danvers ordered her. "Time to go."

Darcy lugged the huge wooden case in her arms through the mailing store. It was now or never—she had to get away.

But Danvers still had one hand around her elbow and the other pointing a gun into her side. If Darcy tried to escape, it would be too easy for Danvers to put a bullet in her. But Darcy was hoping that Danvers would hesitate to shoot her in such a public place. It was her only chance. As soon as she got to the front, she'd make a run for it. She didn't care if the brothers were there. Really, what did she have to lose?

When she got to the front doors, she stopped. "My hands are kind of full. Can you get it?"

Danvers gave her a little snarl as she stepped forward to open the heavy glass door for her. Darcy put her foot out in front of Danvers's ankle, tripping her and throwing her slightly off balance. As she stumbled forward into the opening door, Darcy threw the heavy cylinder container onto her back. Danvers went down. Darcy stepped over her and ran as fast as she could into the parking lot.

TWENTY-FOUR

Before the chopper landed, Ross handed bulletproof vests to both Elijah and Thomas. They donned them, but refused to carry weapons. Thomas didn't even want to wear the vest. The only armor he needed was the Lord's protection. But Elijah gave him a look that said he'd better comply.

The helicopter landed in the far corner of the parking lot of the mailing facility, which it shared with some other not so prosperous businesses. It was a good hundred yards from the front of the store. Ross, Elijah and the two other agents and pilot ran across the asphalt at lightning speed. Thomas moved as fast as he could. With his injured leg, he could not keep up with Elijah or the trained agents. He also heard sirens wailing not so far away. More help was on the way. He just hoped they'd made it in time. He hoped Danvers was here with Darcy. Maybe they still needed the key.

Lord, let us get there in time to help Darcy.

Thomas had prayed over and over. But he feared they would be too late. About thirty seconds after they landed, a large black SUV with its siren blaring pulled into the lot. Another FBI team. It parked much closer to the front of the store. Four men exited. They all carried rifles and wore bulletproof armor.

The few customers that meandered through the lot hurried to move away.

Thomas followed at a distance toward the center of the parking lot.

They were here. Danvers and those twins and Darcy. He could sense it in the air like an evil wind. Ross and his team had not been too late. But where were they? Everything seemed quiet—a little too quiet. No way all of them were inside.

Thomas stood still for a second, just scanning the lot. He spotted movement on the ground between the cars.

"Darcy!"

But then a car engine started behind him. He turned just in time to see a black sedan moving at him at full speed. It was the twins.

"Thomas!" Darcy stood up from between two nearby cars. He looked toward her voice.

"Get down! Get down!" Ross's voice echoed across the parking lot.

Thomas dove between two cars just in time before the black sedan raced across the lane where he'd just stood. Shots rang out through the parking facility. Glass broke. Tires screeched. More shots fired. People in the periphery let out squeals and shouts of fear.

Thomas breathed heavily. He looked under the cars to the left and the right. Finally, he saw her. He tuned out all the chaos around them and then he ran hunched down low to where she hid between the cars.

"Darcy." He knelt down and hugged her to him. She held on to him, burying her head into his chest. "It's okay. You're okay now. It's all over." He stroked her hair. It hung down loose around her shoulders like it had the first day he'd met her. "Thanks to *Gott* this is all over."

She hugged him tighter. Thomas's senses were filled

with her presence. It was over. And he was happy that she was safe.

"Danvers," Darcy said. "She's getting away with the paintings."

"Where?" Thomas said.

Darcy looked around the lot to where Danvers had parked the black Mercedes, just in time to see her slipping into the car with the stolen goods. "There!"

Ross must have been watching them because within seconds, the agent was after Danvers and his team closed in on her. A couple of blown tires later and the whole younger generation of Wissenbergs were in handcuffs.

"All clear!" Ross yelled across the lot. His men had Danvers and the twins apprehended. Darcy couldn't believe it was all over. Thomas had walked her back to a second SUV, which had come to take them home. One of the FBI team had put a blanket around her shoulders and brought her a bottle of water. The others were running damage control in and around the store. A news crew had arrived and was filming in the distance. Agent Ross was escorting Danvers to a police squad car. The helicopter had flown off while an EMS squad had arrived on the scene. It was just like something out of a movie, Darcy thought. One where the good guys actually win.

She sat down inside the vehicle. She still shook and her heart pounded. But she knew it was over. This time it was really over. Another of the team placed the cylinder box from the mailbox at her feet on the floor of the SUV.

"Do you know how to open it?" the man asked.

She shook her head.

"Well, it stays here for now. Keep an eye on it." He winked at them and raced off again to finish questioning people and taking statements.

Darcy looked at the case. The lock was a simple three-digit combination. She ran her hands over the lock. "You think Jesse made this?"

"You can ask him yourself," Thomas said.

"What?" She turned to him, eyes wide.

"Jesse woke up. He's going to be okay," Thomas said. "Blake said he's very weak but that he expects over time Jesse will make a full recovery."

Darcy squealed with delight. She threw her arms around Thomas. How wonderful! All her prayers were coming true.

And Thomas was beside her and that felt good. She knew God had saved her once again. From this day forward she would never live her life the same.

She smiled up at Thomas. "Thank you for coming today. For all you've done, Thomas. You've changed my life."

"Me?" he said.

"Well, yes, you," she said. "Your faith is so strong. And seeing it in you made me want it for myself."

"Then I guess we can thank Jesse for inviting us both over at the same time so that we could meet that day," he said. His grin was beautiful. Everything about him was beautiful. Even his beard, she'd learn to like.

She looked down again at the lock again. "Do you think the combination was in the letter?"

"We can try it." Thomas said. He called out all the three-number combinations that he remembered. Darcy tried each combination accordingly, but the lock remained firmly closed.

"You know, Jesse had my name on the account here," she told him. "That's the only reason Danvers needed me. She found a second key in the wooden box from the well, and her spies in the FBI broke the code from the letter for her, but only an account holder with photo ID would be allowed in the vault."

"I wondered how she was able to open it. We hoped she still needed the key, and would be willing to trade it for you. If she hadn't needed you to get into the vault... I'm glad you're still in one piece."

"Not as glad as I am. But how did she find Jesse?"

"She didn't. Wissenberg did. Remember how Ross said that someone from the US Marshals visited him in prison?"

She nodded.

"Well, Ross's team finally got a name with the face in the video surveillance. It was an older man. Maybe someone that knew Wissenberg before he went to jail. Anyway, he was paid a large sum of money after the third visit to Wissenberg and then he disappeared."

"Do they think he was killed?"

Thomas shrugged. "I don't know, but I'm guessing Danvers got that jacket she was wearing from someone."

Darcy shivered. She pulled the blanket around herself and closed her fingers around it. Her hand brushed the locket. She thought of Jesse. She couldn't wait to see him. She couldn't wait to go back to Willow Trace. She couldn't wait to...

"The locket," she said. "The combination. Of course, it's the date on the locket. Try ten-four. One-zero-four."

He reached down and rolled the combination lock to one-zero-four. It clicked and fell open. Inside was a thick file and about twenty rolled-up scrolls. No wonder it was so heavy.

Thomas pulled out the file and one of the paintings. "What's this?"

They spread the folder and its contents between them. It was a file on Wissenberg. There were pictures of him with different people. And an article about the car crash that her mother had died in. "I think this may connect Wissenberg to my mother's car crash."

"We'll give it to Agent Ross. He'll know what to do with it." Thomas put it aside and unfurled the painting. It was one of the ones in the photos they found in the box.

"It's beautiful," Thomas said.

She looked over at him and they both laughed. "I thought the Amish don't really like art?"

"Well, it's not a necessity so we don't own any. But it sure is beautiful."

"I see you already opened the box." Ross hopped into the vehicle. He lifted the paintings and the files out of the box and secured them in the back of the SUV. Elijah climbed into the front passenger seat. "I know a little Amish wife I just can't wait to get back home to," he said.

"And those paintings will finally go where they belong," Ross said. "To their owners."

"The names on the back of the photos?" Darcy asked.

"Yep, every single one of them," Ross said. "One of our agents just had a quick chat with your father in the hospital. Mostly just to inform him of the seizure of his stolen property."

Darcy was suddenly horrified. "Will he go to jail?"

Elijah smiled. "No. The statute of limitations has well passed, even on this small fortune. Anyway, he has a great defense."

"Really?" Thomas asked. "And what is that?"

"He did it to protect you," Ross said to Darcy.

"What? How would that protect me?"

"Wissenberg knew he kept them. Some of these were paintings he had wanted very badly. And your father told him that he'd give them to him as soon as he got out of jail as long as he didn't harm you," Ross said. "But with two life sentences, I don't think he was ever counting on Wissenberg getting out of jail."

"So why the photos and keeping track of the actual owners?"

"He planned to give the paintings back to them, once Wissenberg passed."

"Or have me do it if Wissenberg outlived him," Darcy said. Thomas had been right all along. Jesse had had reasons. Good reasons. And now they were headed back to see him. She couldn't wait. She could go home now.

But Darcy frowned. Somehow going back to her town house and a life working at Winnefords didn't seem appealing to her in the least.

Thomas sat back in his seat, his eyes falling to the file of pictures and documents they found.

"There was this in the cylinder, too." He passed the folder forward to Elijah. A letter slipped from inside.

Elijah picked it up and handed it to Darcy. "This is to you."

Darcy slowly opened the letter from her father. Thomas watched as her eyes filled with tears.

"Good grief." She wiped her eyes. "I'm like a fountain."

"You had a rough week." Thomas reached over and held her hand. It would be his last chance, but he couldn't mourn that right now. He was too grateful to have the chance at all. He'd been so afraid they would be too late. He was so thankful they weren't.

She squeezed his hand. "It's so sweet. It's just a letter saying that he loves me. And that if I have this letter, then he is gone and he misses me. He tells me that my name was Daria. Daria Rachel Finlay."

"It's a beautiful name. Do you want to be called Daria?"

"No. I'm Darcy now. Can't change that. But maybe one day if I have a daughter..."

Thomas looked away. He didn't want to think about her getting married and having a daughter with someone else. He couldn't have her and he didn't want anyone else to, either. He hated himself for the selfish, possessive feelings he had. He should want her to be happy, even if it meant leaving him behind. And he knew she'd be leaving. She wasn't Amish. He'd simply have to get over his feelings. Just like he had with Mary.

"He wrote more," she said. "Do you want to hear?"

"*Ja*, if you want to share."

"He wrote that he loved me more than anything except God Himself. And that every day he would pray for me to know the love and peace that he'd found in Willow Trace."

Thomas felt his teeth clench. "It must have been a hard way to live, knowing that you were out there and he couldn't see you. Couldn't see you grow up. Couldn't hold you. Couldn't give you his love and protection."

"But no one except for my father knew his burden," Elijah said. "He hid it well. To protect you."

"What will happen to Jesse? Where will he go? His house burned down," Darcy asked. "He'll need someone to take care of him."

"We will rebuild his cottage," Thomas said. "There's already been some talk of starting on it as soon as we get the materials in. And he'll live with me in the interim." Thomas smiled. This way he'd get to see Darcy at least a few times. He knew she would visit her father while he was recuperating.

"But what if I want him to live with me?" Darcy said. "What if I want to take care of him? I'm his daughter."

"You're not Amish," Thomas said. "He took vows. He's not going to go back to the *Englisch*."

"Then I guess I will have to look into becoming Amish."

EPILOGUE

The following September

Darcy had done it. Just like her father before her. She'd left her education, her high-powered job and her town house behind. She'd taken care of Jesse and they'd moved together back into the cottage, rebuilt by the Willow Trace community.

It had all come slowly. At first, she'd just attended Sunday meetings. Then she'd started to learn the songs. She loved the songs. Then she'd learned the Bible, and prayer had become part of her daily life. And Jesse had guided her along. Encouraged her. Loved her. How could she have given up on that?

Darcy had started a sewing business, which she ran from the cottage, performing alterations for both *Englischers* and Amish. Her reputation for perfection and speed had her with an overflow within a few months. So, she expanded to have a turn-around desk at a store in Lancaster, where folks could drop off and pick up items.

In addition, word had gotten out—thanks to Nana Ruth—that Darcy could sew wedding dresses. So now, instead of just making them for Winnefords like she used to do, she made them for brides all over Lancaster County.

Of course, she didn't make dresses for the Amish—Amish women made their own wedding dresses. But since the *Englischers* didn't, she loved making them for many women in and around the Lancaster area who wanted a simple, elegant gown but couldn't afford the haute couture prices of the department stores.

There were some in the Ordnung who disapproved of her business, just as they had of her father's furniture, but times were different now. Most of the Amish were turning from farming to alternate livelihoods in order to survive in today's economy. And really there was no difference in her making a fancy wedding dress than it was for an Amish carpenter to make fancy custom cabinets for an *Englisch* client.

In any case, Darcy shared any extra profit with the community, as Thomas did. And she also had started a mission, where she invited any women who wanted to come to the cottage on Saturday nights and sew with the extra materials that she had left over from the dresses. Working together, they made clothes for the poor. Darcy was pretty sure a few of the older single ladies came to see her father as well as help the poor. But she didn't blame them. He was charming and sweet and everything she'd ever wanted in a father. She could never regret the decision to settle in Willow Trace and become part of his life—especially when it had brought her so many ongoing rewards in her faith and in fellowship with her community.

And all of this had led her to today. Today was a very special day for Darcy. Today was the day she would be baptized in the Amish faith and she would take her vows, just like her father. Everyone would be there—Jesse, Nana, Thomas, Abigail, Blake, Hannah and Elijah. She was shaking both from nerves and from the overflow of joy in her heart. She had baked three apple pies, as there would be a large supper after the service.

Jesse was out hitching his mare to the buggy. She just needed to load up the pies. She saw Jesse through the kitchen window out in the field calling in the horse. Every horse reminded her of that star-filled night with Thomas on the back of the gray plow horse. She'd thought then that Thomas had romantic feelings for her. But since she'd moved to Willow Trace, Thomas had been nothing but a good neighbor.

He was around at Sunday church, barn raisings and the rebuilding of Jesse's cottage. But she probably spent more time with Nana than Thomas. Nana invited Jesse and her regularly to lunch at Nolt cottage and occasionally brought them jars of jam as an excuse to come over and chat. But not Thomas.

Thomas had been different since her decision to stay in Willow Trace. Kind as always. Helpful. But he'd never tried to kiss her again. He'd never asked her to dinner or to go on a buggy ride. She'd once asked Hannah and Abigail if he had another girlfriend. They'd laughed at her and called her silly. But she wondered sometimes, now that she loved Thomas so dearly, did he love her back? Did he ever love her as more than a friend? She had thought so once, but now she was no longer sure.

She dreamed of the one kiss they'd shared. It seemed so long ago. She longed to be in his arms again, but after today, she had vowed to herself, she would move on and stop thinking of him in that way. It wasn't healthy. Anyway, starting today, she would truly become Amish. She could court and she could marry. And if Thomas wasn't the one for her, then God might have someone else, and if not, she was okay with just being Darcy, the Amish seamstress, and living out her life with her father.

Darcy scooped the three pies onto a tray and carried them out to the buggy. Quite a change from her zippy old red sports car. Cars and department stores seemed like a distant memory to her. Sometimes when her friends from work would visit, she would feel a bit nostalgic for her past. But deep down, she knew to have the peace she felt now, she would make this decision a million times over. God had called her to where she was and she was glad to be there. It wasn't for Thomas and it wasn't for Jesse. She did this for God.

Today was about a love that she'd never known before—a love her father had brought to her by getting her to Willow Trace. It was all part of God's design.

Darcy looked across into the north paddock, as she headed toward the buggy. She saw Thomas's horse, King, there in the paddock. Why? Thomas only used King for his own riding when he wasn't using a buggy. And Thomas should have been hitching up his own buggy right that minute to come to her baptism. Did this mean he was not coming? She pushed back a sad feeling of disappointment and hurried on to her buggy.

"A big day for you." Thomas's voice sounded behind her and her heart nearly leaped from her chest.

She stopped and turned around, almost dropping the tray of pies. "Oh, Thomas. You scared me half to death. What are you doing here?"

"Let me help you with those." He reached down and swept the tray from her hands. Their fingers brushed against one another and she hated herself for noticing and liking the way it felt.

"Thanks. I was just taking them to the buggy."

"You should bring a change of clothes, too. Miller's pond is pretty cold. That's where the all the baptisms take place. I was baptized there myself." He took the pies to the buggy and said hello to Jesse, who excused himself into the house. Darcy didn't know which one of them to follow. She chose Thomas.

"You came all the way here to tell me that? Are you not going?"

He walked back to her. His smile was erased from his face, which gave Darcy the strangest, most awful feeling in her gut. And that's when she noticed.

"You shaved. I thought you weren't supposed to shave after you got married. What in the world? That's downright scandalous!"

"You're right. No one shaves after being married." He stopped right in front of her, looking more serious than she liked. He reached up and ran a hand over his smooth chin. It made him look five years younger. But as strange as the beard had seemed to her at first, he now looked silly without it. She could not possibly imagine what would cause him to do something so drastic.

Then a thought came into her head, making her nauseous. He was leaving. Thomas was leaving the Ordnung. Why else would he do such a thing?

"Thomas, what have you done?" She was almost in tears.

Looking confused by her reaction, he tilted his head to the side. "I shaved my beard. I thought you hated my beard?"

"Well, I—I guess I got used to it. Has Nana seen you? What are you trying to do? Put her in her grave?"

Thomas smiled again. "Darcy, slow down. Listen to me. I'm trying to tell you why."

She couldn't breathe. This was it. He was leaving. Why? What had made him decide to do such a thing? She couldn't look at him.

"So, I think you've noticed that I haven't come around much since…well, in months."

She covered her face with her hands to her forehead. Why was he doing this today of all days?

"Well, maybe you did not notice." He shrugged. "But I stayed away because I was waiting to say something to you."

No. No. She didn't want him to tell her that he was leaving. Not today. Not any day. He couldn't leave. She loved him. And she just realized at that moment how very much. She turned away, head down, her hands twisting nervously in front of her.

"Darcy, I can't do this if you turn away. Will you look at me, please?" He reach down and stilled her hands. She turned toward him and lifted her eyes. He smiled down at her and held on tighter to her hands.

"There. That's better."

"I still can't believe you shaved your beard."

"Well…I did it for you. For us. For next month. Did you see how much celery Nana has planted?"

"Celery?" She was about to have a nervous breakdown over his announcement and he was talking about how much celery Nana had planted?

He leaned down and touched his lips to hers. So soft. So sweet. He tasted like apples, just like he had after the fire. He lifted their hands, and then untangled them so that he could touch her face and draw her closer.

"Yes, celery," he whispered, drawing her body into his. "Everyone plants celery when someone in the family is getting married." He kissed her again. "Well, usually it's the bride's family, but Nana was just stepping in for you and Jesse."

"Thomas, I have no idea what you're talking about."

He tried to kiss her again, but she pulled her head back.

"Thomas, seriously. Stop. What are you talking about? Celery? And weddings? And you still haven't told me why you shaved."

"Ja." He kissed her again. "I'm getting to that part." He cleared his throat. "I shaved because it is time—past time—for me to put my first marriage with Mary behind me. I held on to the beard all these years because I was not ready to be a single man again and risk my heart. But you changed all of that." He got down on one knee before her.

"Miss Darcy Simmons, I love you and have for a very long time—so I'm hoping very much that you will agree to be my wife. What do you say?"

She was crying now and nodding. But mostly crying tears of joy. Tears she didn't know how she could ever stop. "I love you, too. Yes, Thomas, yes. Of course, I will marry you."

"Good." He stood, and kissed her again, hard and long, until they were both breathless. "God forgive me, I have wanted to do that since the minute I saw you with your little purse standing on that porch over there."

"Why didn't you?"

"Because I wanted to do it for the rest of my life and at the time, that didn't seem possible. Once you made the decision to come here and live with your father, I could hardly hold myself back... But you still had to decide whether or not to be baptized, and I thought that a lifetime with you might be worth waiting for." He kissed her again. "You don't know how hard it has been staying away from you."

"Please don't ever do it again." She laughed.

"I won't. That I can promise you. And I'll grow my beard back. But this beard is for you. For us."

"Sounds perfect." She put her hands on each of his bare cheeks. "So, now tell me, when were you planning for us to eat all of this celery that Nana has grown?"

He smiled and picked her up into his arms, holding her close. "Well, you tell me… How fast can you make a wedding dress?"

"Pretty fast, Mr. Nolt. Pretty fast."

"*Gutt.* I was counting on that."

* * * * *

If you enjoyed this story, don't miss Kit Wilkinson's other stories of danger and love in Amish country

PLAIN SECRETS
DANGER IN AMISH COUNTRY
"RETURN TO WILLOW TRACE"
LANCASTER COUNTY TARGET

Find these and other great reads
at www.LoveInspired.com

Dear Reader,

Thank you for reading a copy of *Lancaster County Reckoning*. I hope you enjoyed the story of Darcy and Thomas. I was so happy to finally write this story, because I have wanted to do so ever since I started the Willow Trace series. I fell in love the character Thomas Nolt when I was writing *Plain Secrets* and felt like he had to have his own happy ending after having been so good to Hannah in book one.

I dedicated this book to my father, who passed away suddenly while I was working on this book. He was a genius of a man who loved a good story and was a voracious reader. I will definitely miss all of his great advice and chatting to him about my writing.

This book is also dedicated to my oldest sister, who was diagnosed with early-onset Alzheimer's a few years ago. She has spent most of her life taking care of other people, but now depends on others to take care of her. I wish a million blessings to those of you who take care of her—Greg, Charneise, Tamera, Cindy, Mom and my nieces and nephew.

If you or someone you love is suffering from Alzheimer's, my prayers to you.

With all my love,
Kit

Get 2 Free Books,
Plus 2 Free Gifts—
just for trying the
Reader Service!

LIS17R

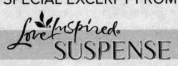
A simple twitch of his finger and his sister's killer would
be gone. His two-month quest to find Van Blackman would
be over. Riley Martelli took one more long look at the man
in his sights then lowered the weapon.

He could never kill someone in cold blood. Not even
the man who'd murdered his sister and put his six-year-
old nephew, Asher, in the hospital with a bullet lodged
near his spine.

Van knelt, but Riley couldn't see what he was doing.
Soon, small puffs of smoke drifted from the patch of
ground.

Riley settled the gun back on his shoulder and got a
better look with the scope. Van crouched over the small
flame, pushing the contents as though trying to encourage
a larger blaze. Riley lowered the weapon again.

Now, in a very secluded area of Colorado's Rocky
Mountain National Park, Van moved to stand next to a
black SUV just a few yards ahead of him.

It might be July in Colorado, but it was cold at night, dropping into the forties. Van wore a black ski cap pulled low over his ears, but his height and broad shoulders were harder to disguise. Riley's heart pounded. Finally, he was going to bring his sister's killer to justice. He shifted the rifle on his shoulder for one more look through the scope. He scanned his prey's body.

His target turned and Riley now had a full-on view of his face—and his heart stuttered.

It wasn't Van Blackman.

Disappointment shot through him. He had the wrong man. Riley lowered the rifle with a frustrated sigh. Then frowned and lifted it to stare through the scope once again. The man's face was familiar. Where had he seen him before? Television? Yeah, that was it. Could it be— He focused again.

Yep. That was the missing FBI agent who had been ali over the news lately. Morrow was his last name. Jake Morrow. And there was a hundred thousand dollars being offered as a reward for his safe return.

Don't miss
BOUNTY HUNTER by Lynette Eason,
available wherever
Love Inspired® Suspense books and ebooks are sold.

www.LoveInspired.com

SPECIAL EXCERPT FROM

Love Inspired®

Nell Stoltzfus falls for the new local veterinarian in town,
James Pierce. But their love is forbidden since he's
English and she's Amish. If Nell follows her heart,
will love conquer all?

Read on for a sneak preview of
A SECRET AMISH LOVE by **Rebecca Kertz**,
available July 2017 from Love Inspired!

"You said your *bruder* was called out on an emergency,"
Nell said. "What does he do?"

"He's a veterinarian. He's recently opened a clinic here
in Happiness."

The strange sensation settled over Nell. Despite the
difference in their last names, could James be Maggie's
brother? "What's his name?" she asked.

"James Pierce." Maggie smiled. "He owns Pierce
Veterinary Clinic. Have you heard of him?"

"*Ja*. In fact, 'twas your bruder who treated my dog,
Jonas."

"Then you've met him!" Maggie looked delighted. "Is he
a *gut* veterinarian?"

Startled by this new knowledge, Nell could only nod
at first. "He was wonderful with Jonas. He's a kind and
compassionate man." She studied Maggie and recognized
the family resemblance. "How is he a Pierce and you a
Troyer?"

"I am a Pierce." Maggie grinned. "Abigail is, too. But
we don't go by the Pierce name. Adam is our stepfather,

and he is our *dat* now." Maggie's eyes filled with sadness. "I was too young to care, but James had a hard time with it. He loved Dad, and he'd wanted to be a veterinarian like him since he was ten. He became more determined to follow in Dad's footsteps."

Nell felt her heart break for James, who must have suffered after his father's death. "You chose the Amish life, but James chose a different path."

"And he's doing well," Maggie said. "My family is thrilled that he set up his practice in Happiness."

Later that afternoon, James arrived to spend time with his family.

She recognized his car immediately as he drove into the barnyard. James stood a moment, searching for family members. Nell couldn't move as he crossed the yard to where tables and bench seats had been set up. Soon, James headed to the gathering of young people, including his sisters Maggie and Abigail.

Nell found it heartwarming to see that his siblings regarded him with the same depth of love and affection. James spoke briefly to Maggie, clearly delighted that he'd handled his emergency then decided to come. She heard the siblings teasing and the ensuing laughter. Maggie said something to James as she gestured in Nell's direction.

James saw her, and Nell froze. Her heart started to beat hard when he broke away from the group to approach her.

Don't miss
A SECRET AMISH LOVE
by Rebecca Kertz, available July 2017 wherever
Love Inspired® books and ebooks are sold.

www.LoveInspired.com